I0736364

Series Titles

Reach Her in This Light
Jane Curtis

The Spirit in My Shoes
John Michael Cummings

Maximum Speed
Kevin Clouther

The Effects of Urban Renewal on Mid-Century America and Other Crime Stories
Jeff Esterholm

What Makes You Think You're Supposed to Feel Better
Jody Hobbs Hesler

Fugitive Daydreams
Leah McCormack

Hoist House: A Novella & Stories
Jenny Robertson

Finding the Bones: Stories & A Novella
Nikki Kallio

Self-Defense
Corey Mertes

Where Are Your People From?
James B. De Monte

Sometimes Creek
Steve Fox

The Plagues
Joe Baumann

Praise for
Reach Her in This Light

"The quiet surface of Jane Curtis's fictional world is all about the roil beneath the surface. Her stories are peopled with women who, though often in dire straits, survive through their quiet abilities—inventiveness, memory, imagination, cheerfulness, strong observation, and humor. Her midwestern characters will evoke women glimpsed on the bus, in the checkout lane. Inhabited as well with animals—dogs and cranes and hawks —and the music of Bob Dylan, these stories are of deep lives in which life arrived to the women "with tumultuous force and carried [them] forward."

—Martha Bergland
author of *A Farm Under a Lake* and *Idle Curiosity*

"Like fragments of colored glass, these brief pieces present glimmering shards of happening, moments of connection in the lives of an intriguing cast of characters who blink in and out of each other's stories, gradually accumulating to combine into a colorfully vivid mosaic of coming of age in the Midwest in the 1960s."

—Christopher Chambers
author of *Kind of Blue* and *Delta 88*

"These spare, linked, beautifully written stories rise like bread into a poetic and moving whole. Whole lives, notably less affluent women's lives, are revealed and celebrated in their telling. At their best, they remind me of the brilliant stories of Tillie Olsen, another writer who probed the depths of generations of working women with grace and feeling."

—Jeffrey D. Boldt
author of *Blue Lake*

"Four resilient women, each finding and flexing her unique voice, come together in Madison, Wisconsin, during turbulent times. Their stories cycle through innocence, hippies, dive bars, poetry and rock music, into gentrification, homelessness, racial trauma and alt-right politics. Despite upheaval, these women are centered and true, never bitter or jaded. They keep on keeping on. They endure husbands dying, lovers who wander in and slip off, a child's untimely passing, adolescent rebellion and skids into poverty. Still, they reach one another and others in the light. As author Jane Curtis quotes wisely, 'nothing is buried in her but is lit and transformed.'"

—Ruth Holladay
The Indianapolis Star

"Each of these stories opens a window into the lives of characters that are often overlooked in the real world. Jane Curtis writes with such insight and compassion that she not only makes it impossible for readers to overlook these characters, she makes it impossible for us to forget them."

—Andy Millman
PLATO Instructor
Madison, Wisconsin

Reach Her in This Light

stories

Jane Curtis

Cornerstone Press
Stevens Point, Wisconsin

Cornerstone Press, Stevens Point, Wisconsin 54481
Copyright © 2023 Jane Curtis
www.uwsp.edu/cornerstone

Printed in the United States of America by
Point Print and Design Studio, Stevens Point, Wisconsin

Library of Congress Control Number: 2023945138
ISBN: 978-1-960329-13-4

This is a work of fiction. Names, characters, businesses, places, events, and incidents are either the products of the author's imagination or used in a fictitious manner. Any resemblance to actual persons, living or dead, or actual events is purely coincidental.

Cornerstone Press titles are produced in courses and internships offered by the Department of English at the University of Wisconsin–Stevens Point.

DIRECTOR & PUBLISHER   EXECUTIVE EDITOR
Dr. Ross K. Tangedal   Jeff Snowbarger

SENIOR EDITORS
Lexie Neeley, Monica Swinick, Kala Buttke

PRESS STAFF
Carolyn Czerwinski, Grace Dahl, Zoie Dinehart, Kirsten Faulkner, Brett Hill, Kenzie Kierstyn, Natalie Reiter, Arianna Soto, Anthony Thiel, Chloe Verhelst

For my mother

Contents

*Some rare battered she-poet, old girl of the Village
racketing home past low buildings some freezing night,
come face to face with that broad roiling river.
Nothing buried in her but is lit and transformed.*

—Muriel Rukeyser, "Breaking Open"

Two Hearts: An Invocation

You always said you had it in you to be a great writer. You needed more experience so it wasn't just a tumble in the orchard, two hearts beating naked between blankets. I felt the potential, the raw power of the river winding through back country. You worshiped the trout, the pebbled underbelly reflecting the stream bottom. When you caught a fish you held it sacred in your hands. You set one trout free. You said he was too big to eat. Then your universe got larger and encompassed the fish in the sea. The trout you released early on was the grandfather of us all.

In college I thought you were too masculine. I thought you formed an enclosed male society and I was decidedly female, hand on the page to forge a woman's literature. But I read you again years later and I see that the power you used to form the words on the page guided me also. You used no exclamation points. Simple. Down there in the water with grandfather trout.

I like to remind myself that we were once on this earth at the same time. You came from Midwest country. I knew the terrain. I like to think we walked the same path. That the Heart was our shared River.

When I was in high school, a strict nun stood in front of the class and explained: "Hemingway's simple prose is deceptive, like the tip of an iceberg. The power is beneath the surface." I could see that this was true. I believed her even though I was already losing my religion. My God was your God, that walk on the path in the back country, those innocent meditations in bed before sleep. I felt so close to you.

I heard my parents talking in the other room. They said you had too much sex in your books and I should not read you. Then they got distracted with their six other children. I continued to hold your words close.

Back in high school I was much too quiet to try to meet you. Now my words flow easily and I wish I would have insisted. I would have been a young girl asking you to reconsider. Go back to Nick. Build on the war years and the loves and the sons. There was still so much to say. It was not only masculine and feminine. You could have had twenty more years. I wish you would lurk deep like that Midwest grandfather trout.

Oh. Here you are streaming through my heart. Guess you meant all along for me to learn through the undertow of words.

"Say Hello"

Eleanor just wanted to throw everything away. She ended up regretting the departure of some books and a green dress. The blue-jacketed pocket-size complete set of Shakespeare's works held no resale value at Half Price Books, so some lucky readers at St. Vinny's got those. She had worn the green dress to her husband's funeral. They were both like that with the greenery, had planted bushes and trees twenty years ago when they bought the house. There were still vestiges of comforting shade for the birds gathered in the side and back yards.

At the funeral people gave her their condolences, but she was too numb to remember much, except that in her mind she summoned up his full name, Raymond, to get his attention. She thought "Raymond, where are you?" But it took her a long time to ever say his full name out loud again. It hurt too much. Her daughter was there, supported by all her middle school friends. The Church Ladies made their funeral lunch: ham sandwiches and baked beans and lime-green Jello with cottage cheese. Everyone talked and remembered, then went back to their own lives.

Right after the funeral, Eleanor's best friend from college and her husband came all the way from Indiana to help the reeling woman snap out of her daze. They had long walks with the dogs. The friend's name was Ruth, but Eleanor gave her the endearing nickname "Root" because their friendship reached deep. Root shared her excitement at acquiring a new daughter-in-law from Thailand, so Eleanor suggested walking to the Thai Pavilion at Olbrich Gardens. The Thai people had donated it to the people of Madison as a gesture of friendship and cultural sharing. They climbed the steps to the top and looked out over Lake Monona, along the way admiring the gold etched into the structure. The very curve of the building spoke of peace and intertwined harmony. At the top the horizon shifted. All people were on Earth at this moment, even though it was twelve hours later in Thailand and people there had already lived most of this day. Root had helped Eleanor make a slow step into the light.

She continued to take backward steps too. Fifty years seemed an unfairly short time to live. She needed to move on, sell the big one-hundred-year-old house. There was no way for her to keep it up. When the house sat on the market for quite some agonizing years, she decided to spruce it up with new bushes as a privacy feature for the backyard. A small local nursery came to dig out the remnants of the old bushes she and Ray had planted together so many years ago. Two young Mexican men started their work. Would she be able to communicate with them? She had decided to scatter Ray's ashes into the ground before they planted new bushes. He would be covered in the shroud of their property. How could she convey such a request? How to ask for some moments of quiet respect when she knew no Spanish? The Mexicans stopped their work when she came out with cans of cool lemonade. They smiled, she smiled. She spoke slowly.

"Would you guys mind taking another lemonade break when you are finished digging, before you begin planting? I need a few quiet moments to remember my husband, scatter his ashes."

She should have known they would understand. The strength of their culture, their honoring of the dead, allowed them to see her need. They smiled, nodded, and agreed. When they knocked at the back door to tell her they were done digging and would take a break before planting, Eleanor was the only family member home, though the family knew what her intentions were that day. Ray's adult son had his own agenda, and it didn't include the second wife. The pre-teen daughter directed her hurt and loss toward mother-rebellion. She had her own ceremony, going with older friends to get a butterfly tattoo to remember her dad always.

It was a breezy fall day, leaves coloring the sidewalk. Eleanor had the box of ashes and knelt to scatter them in the awaiting holes. Suddenly the wind lifted some of the ashes up and they fell like a caress onto her arm. Most of the ashes made it into the holes, yet some scattered across the outreaching red, orange, and yellow tree branches. They had played the Beatles at their wedding, so it seemed only natural for her to sing one final ceremonial song, the one about saying goodbye and hello. She always thought the ending chorus sang "halo" as well as "hello." She sang in full voice. As her tones faded, she thought about what was still there. He flung himself outside the box. He was no saint, but he had an aura of playfulness. A tilted halo.

In the spring she had to give away the house too, in a short sale. Goodbye books, goodbye green dress. Goodbye roof-covered joy. Eleanor moved on. She came back to visit some of her old neighbors and was gladdened to see all the improvements at her old house. The new owners obviously cared about the place. But she was shocked to see that they had taken out the new bushes she had planted and replaced them with a raised vegetable plot. She walked toward the front door. Ray's voice whispered, "Hold on." She decided not to tell the new owners they were growing vegetables on her husband's ashes. This inadvertent discovery was a secret source of freedom. Ray was flying in the wind, and he was tending from the grave.

Other Voices

Amy researched the history of the house before she bought it. She knew she wanted a working-class neighborhood. The house had the distinction of being the first one built on her block, back in 1904, and there was an old water pump in the yard for people and horses to stop, drink, and rest before continuing their journey. She imagined all those who had lived within these walls before, hands helping to pump the water, and then at night those hands gripping the wood banister, telling the stories of their lives to all who wished to listen. Sometimes at night she relived their stories.

Women's voices were especially strong. Most wanted children—others, careers. Amy wanted both, was on the fast track toward punching her time-clock destiny in the gut. She had spent her fertile years reinventing herself: anthropologist, collector, protester, poet. By the time she met George, she had finally gotten around to her biology, looking at life through the lens of pistils and stamens. Tendrils, the longing for a child, surfaced from some underground roots and a flower begged to be put into being. George, for his part, seemed cautiously eager to oblige. She had met and eventually married him when he moved to her neighborhood in Madison from New Haven. He introduced himself as a former Yale hanger-on who had suddenly needed to break free from Ivy League walls. He stood on her front porch often, once in a fist-raised steel workers T-shirt. Amy sensed the lure in his political stance. They discovered a similar bond in struggles against class distinctions, she with her work to create new paths for women, he with his Wobbly Industrial Workers of the World union-building.

For a year they dealt with practical biology: timing and temperature. The effort started to wear thin. Where was the romance? In bed Amy turned to George and whispered a word in his ear: adoption. She imagined the sound swirling down his ear canal. Maybe their family existed, and they just hadn't met the baby yet. George was restless in sleep. In the morning he stretched and protested. They were too old. Their records were less than perfect. Could a fit parent have an arrest record for picketing? Adoption required more stringent rules than a young couple throwing caution to the wind. Amy pleaded her case: "Some young, frightened woman may be looking for an older couple." Her voice must have sounded emphatic. She could hear the pounding in his ear canal when he finally said "yes."

They discovered that the battle had just begun. The primly dressed social worker sat behind her desk, ready to navigate through the bumpy road ahead. There were fees to pay, physicals to pass, biographies to write, photographs to put in an album, letters of recommendation to request, a home inspection, and an inevitable wait which the social worker warned them would be triple nine months or longer. Then she said something in a rapid-fire drum tap voice: "You'll never move up the list for a white child. Consider foreign adoption, or a Black infant Stateside. Whichever way you choose, you may wait for a child who never arrives."

Amy looked at George. The woman wasn't telling them anything they didn't already know. The two nodded in agreement. Silence. George couldn't seem to get his words out.

Amy knew from her inner reeling body that it was because years ago as a young husband and father he had lost his only child in a house fire. She had never met Jenny, but George had shown her a photograph of him brushing out his daughter's long blonde hair. It had taken years for George to even talk about the trauma. The loss had destroyed his first marriage. Silence became his way to cope. One night several years into their marriage George had finally been able to describe the void to Amy: "Ashes burn the remnants of who I am." She knew that another child could never replace Jenny, yet she had to try and light the way for him. Amy worked her commiseration with George's plight into their response to the social worker: "We would honor and cherish an African-American baby, raise a strong self-identified child." George said, "We're ready to take on the shared cultures." His voice sounded gruff, as if it reached the surface from some inner chamber of accumulated grief.

Back at home, the poet in her tried to salvage George from his great loss by suggesting that he start with painting the room for the nursery. She knew they needed to get practical with their efforts. They poured over swatches of paint and decided on a pale green called "Glisten," shades of grass in the dawning light. The brush strokes had a certain calming effect.

Then Amy got busy with the letters of recommendation. She asked Sally, her old neighbor, a stalwart in the community. She had babysat Sally's four kids all the years they were growing up, starting back when Amy was in eighth grade. They met for lunch at Atlas Café and ordered their usual tea and pancakes. After Sally had drizzled apricot syrup over her pancakes, she looked at Amy: "Every child is unique. Look at how different my kids are. A mix of introverts and extroverts." Her dear old neighbor smiled. "Even as a young girl you knew how to bring out the best in each of them. I will say so in my letter." Amy sipped her tea and felt a warm glow emanating from the artful display of maple syrup on her pancakes. The first bite tasted like renewal. Her doubts about the possibility of success began to disappear. Sally's wise perspective forged Amy's growing sense of hope.

She proofread George's recommendation request to his boss at union headquarters. He sounded organized and forthright. Amy swelled with pride for his determination in the face of all that he had battled through. She wrote to the professor in charge of the Writing Workshop where she taught older adults how to hone their skills. Amy had received many high evaluations from her students. The professor mailed her a reassuring response: "I told the adoption agency (based in Texas, really! How near and yet so far!) that your students love you." In this new light of an eventual successful adoption the excited couple kidded around with photographs for the album, which came together playfully with silly hats. To show another side of their relationship, on one page they wore solemn expressions in the pew of a church. George even toned that one serious photo down by wearing a plain T-shirt. He even took his hat off. They did not include any photos from the tragedy of the past.

The social worker was right about the wait. Doubts surfaced again. Every nine months or so Amy felt her gut drop a little lower, a physical reaction to a rising fear of failure. George was restless in bed most nights, his side of the bed wet with sweat. She held him close, combed his hair with her fingers. "Don't worry, we will survive."

One night, about three years into the wait, Amy startled awake in the black of night. George seemed to be sleeping peacefully for the moment. Her side of the bed felt as damp as his. She decided to go downstairs for fresh air and refrigerator water. She leaned onto the handrail and felt the presence of all the other women who had used this old wood banister. The past voices spoke to her: "Hold on. We're *here*." Amy saw physical reminders too. When she bought the house a woman from the past had painted the staircase pink. She wanted to turn the house into a jungle gym for her kids. George had spent many hours restoring the staircase to its original wood. Another woman had allowed her moody daughter to paint her own bedroom. The room was a blackand-blue bruise. Amy worked to bring the light back.

At the bottom of the stairs, she turned toward the kitchen, and in the darkness of that turning she saw George's hand brushing Jenny's long blonde hair away from her face, distinctly heard a young girl's voice say: "I'm fine. I'm wisps of air following you." The image faded when she opened the refrigerator, but Jenny's words reverberated in the dim light of the door.

Amy sat on the front porch rocker drinking her water. As she went back and forth in the rocker, she could hear her old house sigh with the secrets of past voices. A breeze blew through her mind. Thoughts of Jenny had given her a revival of spirit. Awe was in the air. Somewhere in this universe an infant, their infant, was whispering from the darkness of a womb, waiting to be born.

Little Shoe Box

Louise tried to hide her swelling belly with big sec-ondhand men's shirts. Everyone treaded around her, whispering. When the baby announced herself to the world, she was sickly, her cry no more than a whimper. The powers that be said it was because she was two months early. Louise was content to quit college and care for her girl. What good would a few English classes do in the scheme of things? She rejected all the usual family names, those echoes of traditions, and named her daughter Lola. It sounded like a feisty name, a name that would punch away at the grit of their impoverished life. The baby's father had not wanted to be in the picture and refused paternal obligation. He said she slept around, and she didn't want her mother to hear more of his accusations. Louise's mother was aghast at her loose behavior. Even one sin was too much. Siblings turned their backs.

If only she could work to keep her small, ramshackle apartment. But the care of Lola took all her time. Emergency room bills added up. It cost many dollars just to walk through the door. The hospital demanded a monthly payment schedule. She couldn't meet anyone's needs. The landlord, an older man named Hugo, sent her an eviction notice. Her nerves quivered to the surface and the letter shook. When she crumpled the paper in frustration and threw it across the room it embodied a lost creature far away from home. Mother and daughter were going down fast.

Hugo stopped over to inspect the apartment, assess damages, and decide if she would get her deposit back. She didn't like the way he leered at her, as if she were a wayward woman. She clung to the innocence of Lola. Louise tried to show her spirit, reminding Hugo that it wasn't her fault the shower didn't have enough water pressure. He rolled his eyes and looked at her with deceitful sympathy. His hand lingered a little too long on her shoulder.

"I'm going to give you a break. Pay me $270 dollars a month and you can stay for a while. You can work the rent off in my real estate office, bring your baby along." He said it like he was doing her a great favor. She was up late most nights with the threat of "for a while" ringing in her head. She needed stability for her daughter. He had that man-speak control in force. Louise had witnessed men who ignored women's voices, told the world how to live. When man-speak reared up, no honesty could survive. Her former boyfriend had done the same thing. There had to be a way to unhinge their grip. She struggled in the night to get away from the hold of their torment.

Louise was nervous when she applied for some disability insurance; a lot of people used lawyers, but she didn't have the money. She was told it would take a lot of time to get to Lola's case. She heard horror stories about strict rules for eligibility. She tried to make the hospital and apartment payments. Lola had short spurts of growth, so small for a three-year-old toddler that the emergency room nurses nicknamed her "sweet pea." Medical bills skyrocketed. Hugo started to get more and more impatient. His hands began to linger longer, moving around different parts of her body.

Louise didn't know how to make the hands stop. Man-speak clanged around in her head and warned her to move on.

She decided to give the Salvation Army a try. In her interview with the crisply dressed captain, she liked that he did not mention "onward Christian soldiers" even once. He showed them to their assigned beds and Louise thought "maybe at this place we can be who we are." There was a roof. There was running water. There was a food pantry. Louise watched Lola toddle pajama-clad and barefoot around the rows of neatly made army cots, the mother in her wrestling with the memory that her girl had turned over in sleep and broken her wrist.

At Christmastime a smiling-faced bell ringer befriended them.

The woman glanced down into her kettle drum. "I'm a member of the finance committee. There's a bit more money coming in this time of year. So, we're going to give you gifts. You have to promise to wait 'til Christmas morning to open them." The woman's eyes sparkled. Louise thought all that bell ringing must have chimed awake the woman's refreshing outlook on life. She held Lola close, hoping her child was feeling that same energy.

The Salvation Army shelter staff made an effort at celebrating Christmas: red ribbons and green garlands, the scent of pine. A lot of the people were already out on the streets for the day. Louise sat Lola next to her on the cot, watched her feet dangle down in an endearing way. She gave Lola her sparkling foil-wrapped gift and the child tore into it. She sat with a little shoebox on her lap, lifted the lid, pushed aside the tissue and held up a sweet pair of shoes. The bell ringer must have secretly measured Lola's feet; the pink leather shoes looked like just the right size. Lola squealed with delight and begged to have Louise put them on her right away. She began her wobbly march around the army cot, kicking the little shoebox as if it were a ball. Kids could invent toys out of anything! Was Lola going to play her game without falling and really hurting her weakened bones? Louise offered up a hopeful prayer to whatever god was looking down. That vague god had let them down for Lola's first pair of Goodwill baby shoes, the ones that made her feet look like oversized wigwams.

Now it was Louise's turn. She supposed it would be something practical to ward against the cold months ahead. Instead, she lifted out a fife, a smaller, higher pitched version of a flute. How thoughtful! She blew her first breaths into the mouthpiece. The trill that came out reminded her of early morning birds, and the bird calls made her want to go outside. Mother struggled to put a coat on her daughter, took her hand, coaxed her out to join the people on the streets. She hoped walking in the wind would strengthen Lola's legs. Louise carried her fife in her other hand for comfort. A chorus of birds conducted a concert against the wintery air, urging them onward.

Lola was already tiring, so Louise chose a nearby park bench on which to rest. Street people were milling about. She supposed they were looking for adventure, or perhaps just some kind of comfort. An old street guy came limping along, a dog at his side. Mother and daughter scrunched over to make room for him on the bench. His dog sat obediently at his feet. Louise noticed there was no leash. That's the way street people liked to live, no strings attached, no puppet control. Vagabonds savored the pure frigid breath of freedom.

The dog gave Lola a lick of a kiss on her leg, and she moved her legs back and forth, made the bench into a swing. Louise hoped the dog's kiss had given Lola enough strength for the walk ahead. The old man looked at them with penetrating eyes: "This here is Wally, my lifelong friend." Louise scratched Wally behind his ears, letting the dog smell the story of who she was. His wet nose felt like a revival. Lola placed her wrist next to the dog's nose and he did the same with her. They thanked the old man for sharing Wally with them, used their renewed energy as a bulwark against the bitter wind, got back to the Salvation Army. That night Lola wanted to sleep in her new shoes. Louise thought it would be okay. She played her fife until the "lights out" call.

Over time the music wasn't enough to ward off the cold air. It permeated the walls and invaded Lola's lungs, compromised her bones. The doctors in the emergency room offered little hope. Her lungs had been rattling since birth. Louise held Lola's hand, lay her head on Lola's chest, tried to breathe into the slowly rising and falling cavity to bring her around, but, right there in the emergency room, her lungs were a gurgle of bye-bye. She held Lola for the last time, whispered her own version of "Hello, Goodbye." The toddler shoes lay motionless in the sorrow of the sluggish hospital air.

She chose a simple casket, a little bigger than a box that could hold adult boots. The bell ringer helped her get through the funeral. She even helped pay for the burial. Louise often wished she could escape the rattle of her daughter's lungs. She tried to fill her mind with the bell ringer's name. But the rattle was overpowering. If only she had asked the name of the older guy on the park bench. She did remember the dog's name: "Wally," the creature who had given them comfort when they needed it. Much of the rest of that winter was a blur. Maybe it was better that she remembered the bell ringer and the old guy as the ones who chimed in with creative gifts, gifts that encouraged play: a little box containing a pair of shoes, a fife, the comfort of a dog's wet nose.

Was she selfish to keep the gift of those shoes? Lola wouldn't need them anymore and she needed to carry Lola with her. On a spring night she stuffed one shoe inside each of her raincoat pockets, walked away from the Salvation Army, vowed to devote herself to the people living on the streets. Louise sat on the very same park bench, the one she and Lola had shared with the old homeless man and his dog. She played her fife into the sudden unleashed rain, defying God or anyone else to ever hurt her again.

Troubadour

The senior citizens arrived with canes and walkers for their healthy noon meal. By serving them Maddy found herself learning dignity in the menial. Plus, she got a free meal out of the deal. She reveled in the pleasure of tasting the community of flavors. She hoped her volunteer work might bring her out of her own self-imposed isolation.

Joyce, the food service director, was a role model. She began each meal with a group activity: Plant a seed. What are your baseball memories? Let's listen to Hank Williams. What is your favorite song of all time? She empowered each of the challenged seniors. The older minds gyrated in mental gymnastics.

After the meal, after the clattering of plates and pans in the sink, Maddy would sit down with Joyce and make plans for the days ahead. Bingo. Group Jeopardy. Did you save baby teeth? Yours? Your children's? Does the Tooth Fairy exist? The two women got to be quite close, sharing family sagas as well as thoughts for future activities. One day she noticed Joyce clutching her arms around herself, head swaying. Something was amiss.

"Gosh, Joyce. Why so down? How's everything at home?"

A big sigh. A gulp of courage. "Fred has left me and the boys for a younger woman. All of a sudden. Snap. Just like that."

Joyce haltingly told her the details, admitted she had not seen the jilt coming. Their marriage was the age-old tale of an older boss and young secretary. Both philosophized about men and their mid-life crises. Or, as the friends would later understand, their second childhoods. Over the next few weeks Maddy witnessed Joyce climb out of her hole, go back to school, improve.

Maddy began to notice jilts all around. Newspaper headlines screamed of a love child breaking up many marriages: politicians, the wealthy, no one was immune. Where do older women put the pain? She had an inkling that question would soon descend into her very being. It left a sour taste in her mouth. A young woman who lived around the corner had been sashaying by.

She arrived home from her volunteer role pondering the quirks in life. Stuart was glued to his usual television program. For days he had seemed remote; the control was elsewhere. Maddy decided to reason with him. Didn't men like logic and reason? She stood between Stuart and the television and made a declaration.

"After all our years together, I think we've built a solid foundation. We don't want to go into old age with crumbling hearts. You know, like the Beatles song about being sixty-four."

Stuart looked at his watch. "I've got the blah-des."

She could see him fading into a blank screen.

During all the years of their marriage Maddy had found it difficult to part with words, had built her own private castle. She saw the chasm grate on Stuart. She wanted to tell him that the volunteer job had begun to unlock her voice. But Stuart was already gone, swept in the tumult of that young woman around the corner. For a while Maddy wallowed in a silent abyss. At the senior meal site, she merely plopped food on the plate. Nothing tasted appealing. Then Joyce came up with raucous sing-a-longs for a new activity. The group sang with such heart they could have been in the deep mysterious caverns of a karaoke bar instead of the community room in low-income senior apartments. Maddy's voice began to emerge from a long sleep.

The cafe in her neighborhood beckoned. She sat alone over a steaming cup, relished the dip of a raspberry scone into her coffee and allowed her combustion of loss and loneliness to explode. Her voice croaked a lament from the depths of a teeming emotional bog.

"St-u-art. Love is in ruins. The deal's going down."

Ruins. Rue the day. Her strange thoughts and sounds filled the air. The heads of the people at the next table turned. There were no cards in front of her, nothing material to be dealt. Stuart had left a void that could only be crossed with laments. She sung out her pain. Maddy didn't care if she was creating an awkward moment. A patron from that jovial table came over to sit with her, a look of concern on her face.

"Can I get you a refill on your coffee? Or perhaps you've had too much caffeine?"

"I'm exactly fine. I need to sing out my words. Stored inside too long a knocked around life."

The woman looked at her and nodded. "I'm Eleanor. Been coming here for coffee for years. We all need to get words out in the open. Uncover. Discover."

Maddy saw the power in Eleanor's eyes, felt confidence in the stability of the coffee shop table. Joyce and the senior citizens and all the people sitting here were waiting, anticipating, and, yes, some perhaps dreading to hear her songs. She hummed "London Bridges Over Troubled Waters".

She looked down at her plate and found to her astonishment substance, not garnish. Right there, nestled against the crumbs of the scone, was a thin slice of cantaloupe. Café Zumba had presented her a card to play, handed to her through the happenstance of a piece of fruit. That old poker song somersaulted into her mind, the one about knowing when to hold, when to fold.

Maddy's breath rushed in and came back out. And again.

She spoke: "We find the best deals in a slivered moon-shaped slice of cantaloupe. I savor the sweet melon on my tongue."

Maddy took her moon image, handed her fertile craziness to this new friend Eleanor, who seemed delighted with the new way of appreciating the moon. "Now it's time for me to go." Her invented lyrics would be easier to practice if she left the coffee shop and started walking home. She sounded out loud along the bike path. "Love is in my soul. The weeping willow dries her tears and bursts green buds. You cannot take my soul away."

A halo of the "o!" sound from "hold" and "love" and "soul" hung in the air, the gentle weep of a Beatle guitar and an exclamation of recognition both at once. The castle she had built up was a distance behind her. She cast her lure of words, strummed her troubadour lyre. The purple haze of the sky kissed her on the lips and she smiled. Clouds inverted.

"Hold on love." She folded into herself.

The bicyclist coming up from behind cut a wide path around her and rang his bell. He smiled at her as he passed by. She realized by instinct that he was not avoiding her, just giving her space. Eleanor had done the same.

The bicyclist looked back over his shoulder. The wind pushed his long kinky beard to one side. She saw purple in his eyes. She saw his mouth catch the energy of her lyrics: "Hearts afire!"

At that moment Maddy knew her own words were going to save her.

Mr. Bojangles

He was a fixture on Madison's State Street for years. The street people knew him as Mr. Bojangles, the window washer. His dog Wally was always at his side. Louise watched him accept change for his labor and always feed Wally first. The dog had no need for a leash.

Mr. Bojangles carried his long-armed squeegee across his chest like a bayonet, a soldier following marching orders, the pistol of Windex tucked in his belt. Louise sometimes played her fife to match his marching beat. Every window on State Street needed attention. He would wash the window first, then venture inside to seek whatever payment the retail owner deemed appropriate. Wally would wait right by the front window until the love of his life returned.

Louise liked to scratch Wally behind the ears, but she couldn't distract the dog from the object of his affection. She was glad they had their strong bond, but worried about them, worried about all the street people, when the cold cried out for a Three Dog Night.

The windows on State Street glistened in the sun. Mr. Bojangles branched out to the Capital Square and the contemporary art gallery. He squeegeed until the vases and jewelry shone. He and Wally stopped to rest on a bench near the Capital Lawn. Louise invited herself to sit next to them.

"Guess you know that everyone appreciates your elbow grease."

"Ya. Well. A man needs to exist."

She reached over to scratch Wally, who tolerated her. She began to read the book that Mr. Bojangles wrote with his eyes.

"Where do you sleep at night?"

"Oh. Here and there. Front porches. Heating grates. Sometimes right up here on the   Square."

Louise knew what he was going through, felt with a shudder the memory of her life on the streets. She had taken college courses in English. Then her daughter's medical bills had pushed her out of her apartment.

"For a long time I thought I'd never be able to jump off the runaway train of poverty. But now I'm looking for some low-income senior housing." Mr. Bojangles' eyes danced skyward. "Give me air and freedom any day of the week." His voice swam in lush waters.

Louise found out she could live under a roof and still be free. With her new housing location on the eastside of Madison, she didn't make it up to State Street very often anymore. She liked sitting at the picnic table in her own backyard listening to Dinosaur Rock on her portable radio. She had found Rip, an old hippie who liked the same 1970s music.

One day Louise and Rip took a bus down to Capital Square to enjoy the Fall colors. She saw Mr. Bojangles slumped down on a bench. There was no Wally anywhere. She gently put her hand on Mr. Bojangles' shoulder. He looked up. His eyes were deep oceans. The old lament about the dog dying wound its way through her mind. She tried to break the grief in the air.

"I'd like to introduce you to my friend Rip. He'll appreciate your handiwork with the windows."

Rip stood with his back to the shimmering vases and raised his hand. A wave swelling from the depth of an ocean passed through the two men.

Mr. Bojangles looked into the distance.

"I always leave a smudged nose signature in the lower corner."

She watched his oceans become fathoms. He pointed an arthritic finger. His voice did a little shaky dance.

"Here's Wally coming over the hill."

Louise knew from memory that wishful feeling of listening for footsteps that never arrived. Her daughter Lola had gurgled her last breath years ago. Lola lingered on. Wally lingered on. She thrust her hands deep inside her jean pockets. She felt the little dog biscuit she had brought along to try and be a better friend to Wally. Her right fingers crushed apart the treat. When she reached to give Mr. Bojangles a hug, she tugged her inside pockets out. The crumbs of the biscuit fed the hovering air.

The Bully

Eleanor braced herself every time the city bus ground to a halt in front of Visions nightclub, the only stripper bar in town. It was a stop that could cough up various questionable cads. The bus waited long enough for her to read the large sign on the front of the building: "NO SAGGING." For a long time she didn't know what the sign meant. Then one day two women sitting in front of her discussed the sign. She found out it meant "don't wear your pants too low." She started seeing gang members of all races proudly showing their cracked asses.

One sunny day on the bus she heard teens bullying an old woman, calling her "hag ass" and "fatty fat" and "dinosaur fossil." She had known there was going to be trouble the minute the teens got on the bus at the Visions stop. The ringmaster's cracked ass was a red flag. He led his gang in a rap of ridicule. She saw the old woman put on her mask of oblivion, slump down in her seat. She interpreted the mask to mean "don't intervene, I've heard it all in my long life." Eleanor had heard it all before too, and in this case she regretfully decided not to jump into the gang fray, found herself a seat further back on the bus. Best to play it safe in a saggy situation.

The cranky old engine's halt and start sounds gave her time to go back over the clamor of memory. She loosened the blue scarf which was her refuge against the first onslaught of

Wisconsin's fall weather. The incident with the old woman brought back a scene from her own life.

Her husband Ray was already facing a serious illness and she wanted to distract their daughter Alice from the gloom of home. Mother and daughter went to the zoo, laughed at the antics of the seals and polar bears. Eleanor decided that a children's restaurant would be a fun place to have lunch. There was a clown balloon man working the room, twisting the bouncy shapes into animals to delight the kids. It was their turn and the exaggerated yellow upturned lips and polka-dot cheeks stood in front of them. He made her daughter a twisted puppy dog, her favorite animal. Then he stood in front of Eleanor and blew up two balloons and held them up to her bosoms. "Hubba-Hubba" came from behind his menacing lips. Then he walked away.

The start-up sound of the bus engine made Eleanor aghast all over again at the misogyny in the clown's gesture. Alice was eight and kids were already being warned about bullying at school. Even at her young age they talked about the indicators of bullying in their family conversations. Ray was never one to put up with any guff, even after he got so sick. Alice took a fork, slammed it down hard into the bouncy surface, and destroyed her balloon puppy. The popping sound disturbed the room, but only momentarily. Both mother and daughter understood the lingering magnitude of the derision in the clown's leering gesture and wanted everyone in the room to be aware. They hadn't ordered lunch yet, and they left the restaurant in a huff, warning the young family at the next table on their way out, Alice shaking her head in disgust, Eleanor saying the warning loud enough for others to hear:

"That clown is a social menace. Don't be fooled by his smiling face."

The families looked surprised, but she was glad she had sent out a radar warning.

The bus lurched forward and called up the memory of her girlfriend having breast reduction surgery. The girlfriend had then looked slender enough to slide down the straw in a Diet Coke commercial. Ray had said "Don't you dare." She could still hear the muscle of love in his voice. From that moment on she was proud and would never change the gift she had inherited from her stout grandmother. Ancestry crafted her body and her words. Perhaps her daughter would inherit these gifts too. She needed to pull off the circus mask of frivolity on this interfering clown. Eleanor talked with Alice about the incident. Bullies could cloak themselves in many obtrusive ways. She needed to talk about their subtleties. Kids emulate their parents before they get into their rebellious phase and then come out on the other side.

"That clown was completely offensive. How dare he come anywhere near me with those mocking words and gestures. We need to put a bully in his or her place."

She knew that lunch was imperative after their long walk through the zoo. She promised Alice she would call management at the restaurant and complain about the bully. If nothing was done she vowed to write a letter and take it to the higher-ups. Go see the CEO in person. She wrapped one arm around her midriff and the other around her daughter. They leaned in towards each other, embracing who they were becoming.

"Mom. Mom. We are lucky to be us." Alice's voice sounded strong.

They went on a carousel ride at Bev's restaurant, a fun kid place just down the block where the atmosphere was more carnival than circus. They enjoyed lunch. Both learned from the experience and were comfortable in the flow of their bodies.

The bus pulled away from the curb and the sound of the resurgence made Eleanor go forward in her memory. As she matured Alice did begin to inherit her generous body from the stout grandmother. She told Eleanor she knew who she was and declared herself happy with that cherished first boyfriend.

They went through the agony of watching their loved one deteriorate. Ray died when Alice was in eighth grade. They grieved. They remembered. They moved on. Neither of them allowed the clutch of grief to consume them.

Bev's had to dismantle their carousel due to safety reasons and Alice and Eleanor found inventive ways to play, listening to what animals were telling them as they trounced around the zoo, even when Alice was in high school. A different animal became the main attraction each time. They shared the luxury of spreading their wings like a flamingo, vowed to eat shrimp to be as pink as possible. A favorite place was the new zoo restaurant window that showed the polar bears at play in their own deep pool of water. One seemed to say to the other watch me dive deeper than you, feel me somersaulting, go over, put a paw on your shoulder. Mother and daughter appreciated the massive grace of their playful swimming, agreed the polar bears loved each other. She remembered the feeling of joy on the carousel when she put her hand on Alice's shoulder.

The sagging gang swaggered off the bus, the white bullies thinking they were in control but they were not. The law was starting to identify their atrocities, whatever race they happened to be. A few stops later Eleanor pulled the cord to get off. She wrapped her scarf around her throat, gently looped the blue pattern around her exposed neck. The clown incident stayed with her. She swayed back and forth down the aisle of her memory. She passed by the old woman and stopped to face her. She gave her a reassuring smile.

"Don't let the bullies get to you. They come sneaking through many people's lives. They need to be banned. Convicted."

She said the final word with such force that the woman held her head higher up. She took off her mask and smiled.

The Mother

What would happen if one woman told the truth about her life?
The world would split open

—Muriel Rukeyser, "Kathe Kollowitz"

Eleanor looked next door in disgust. Her old conservative neighbor had a "Support Police" sign stuck in the ground out front. She took a gulp of air and quickly walked a few blocks to try to let off steam. Today's anniversary would not allow the steam to escape.

She got to Williamson Street and could feel the tremors of the crowd. People were bouncing their anger off of each other. The bereaved mother stood in the incongruous sun and used a bullhorn to ask for a calm day of service to the community. Eleanor could hear her words. She could hear the truth of her journey from grief toward healing amplified through the bullhorn. She wanted to honor the mother, honor her son, Tony, the young Black man shot dead by the police. They all stood milling around the house where he had died one year ago today.

She saw people of all ages joined together in common sorrow. The Young Gifted and Black from the local high school. Some well-dressed people on their lunch break. An old hippie couple. The hippie woman had her arm hooked around an even older shriveled gentleman whose eyes looked intently at the grieving mother.

The periphery of the crowd afforded the best views. Eleanor could see the altar of flowers and notes and stuffed animals on his former front porch. The mother seemed to want a sacrificial dignity. The police made their presence known along the edges of the crowd. Eleanor noticed next to her an older woman, pale, upset, clearly leaning against a young Black woman in tears. The pale woman leaned over to wipe away tears and console the young woman. Eleanor heard her words of constrained grief.

"I know this is difficult." She called the young woman Gwen. "We need to honor Tony's mother."

"Yes. Yes. But it is so unfair."

Then their voices drifted away in the rush of the crowd during the makeshift memorial service. Mostly the mother used a bullhorn to talk about her loss. Eleanor kept hearing her truth. "STOP. CONTAGION." The mother's words split open a festering wound. Time for the healing that Tony could have given.

The mood was heady with the power of the united crowd. The memorial was over and the police moved for dispersal. One of their own had shot the young man dead. Eleanor thought there is no justice in this world. She wanted to right the wrong, split it in half, bring us back together in a new way. For the last year the police seemed to want it too. They were out in the neighborhood more. It could be the beginning of a healing.

People were starting to leave. An elbow jabbed her in the side.

"Sorry. Sorry. I got pushed into you."

It was the pale woman who still had the Black woman standing next to her.

"That's okay. I'm fine. I feel so bad though . . . any human contact is a good thing . . ."

"Oh. I know what you mean. I'm Amy and this is my daughter Gwen."

"Eleanor." Was it who she was? She felt unsteady and struggled for reclamation. "Just trying to figure out what community service I can give."

Amy smiled and nodded. "That's the power of the mother speaking. Do you want to go over to Café Zumba and get some tea?"

Eleanor was glad she had been offered the olive branch of friendship. "Sure. That would be fine. I need to get off my feet."

The cozy space was jumping but they found a spot upstairs. The three of them sat over steaming tea and a split scone. Gwen excused herself to go carry protest signs with her Young Gifted and Black friends. Tony had been a little older, but the young kids could feel his presence in the high school halls, knew that one trigger happy policeman had destroyed much promise. Amy nodded in her direction.

"She's a big part of my contribution. Yet she has given me so much more."

Eleanor smiled. "I wish I could think of what I could give . . ."

"Well, you're here on the street making your opinion known."

Eleanor looked at her new friend. "I guess I'm supposed to try to put the community back together after the shooting." The enormity of the task stood in front of her like a stone wall.

Amy squeezed her hand. "You need to start small. Do one thing for one person."

The two women clinked tea cups, admiring the delicate flowers painted on the vessels of their friendship before Eleanor offered, "Let's exchange phone numbers. Or do you prefer e-mail?"

The sky had lowered on the brightness of the day. It seemed appropriate for the somber occasion. They left Café Zumba walking east. It was then that Eleanor saw the old hippie couple sitting on a bench at the bus stop with that same older gentleman. The hippie woman held a battered radio on her lap. Mick Jagger was making nostalgic howls in the background. The hippie guy was swaying to the sound. The slumped older man looked at her and she practically swam in his intent eyes. The world opened up to possibility. The old man took out a ragged handkerchief and started rubbing out the smudges on the glass surrounding the bus shelter.

Eleanor now knew what she needed to do. She hooked arms with Amy before they parted to go in different directions. When she got home she saw her wrinkled, conservative neighbor, knees on the ground, working with gloved hands to pull weeds from her vegetable garden. She walked over in the dusk, knelt down to help her with the task.

Like a Hurricane

Maddy thought she needed to move to Florida and live in a swamp. Her alligator eyes were bulged from crying. Men had a habit of upping and leaving. Maybe there was a good-hearted codger down south who was looking for love. She said goodbye to her best friend Eleanor, bought a ticket, hopped a train to Florida, sleeping upright all night. The chugging of the train, the caress of the motion, made sleep surprisingly easy.

She awoke to a strange world of cotton and tobacco fields and, after several more hours, palm trees. She alighted from the train, pulled a small wheeling suitcase, and hailed a taxi to her pre-arranged rental in a trailer community near the Gulf in southern Florida. They had mailed the key to her ahead of time, so she was able to walk right in.

With a community pool and a grocery store nearby, she would be self-sufficient. Social Security was already deposited in the branch of her bank located there. She had not had a car in a long time and wouldn't need one now. She felt freer than she had in years, had gotten away from the man who devoured her heart, clogged her troubadour voice. All her sad songs sat in the folds of her throat.

One day a man came walking toward her. Maddy made the gutsy move of saying "Hi." The man stopped and they chatted briefly about the weather in Florida. His name was Ralph and he was a native Floridian.

"It's fine for now, but watch out for the fall hurricane season. What you need to do is get out of Florida, relocate northern inland shoals ahead of time. Look for shallow river banks. The Gulf and the Atlantic possess the power to swell above your head." His voice had an edge to it. "Another caution: if you're headed toward the Everglades watch out for snakes and alligators. They'll make a snack of you."

This new Ralph person then recounted a true story from the previous night's local news about a twelve–year-old girl's battle with an alligator. The beast was pulling the girl under, under, shaking her back and forth in his mouth, anticipating his tasty morsel. Ralph paused for dramatic effect. Maddy was caught up in the horror of his story. It became a huge gift for her when Ralph said that the girl had the presence of mind to stick her fingers in the alligator's nostrils. The beast had to open his mouth to breathe and the girl escaped.

Maddy grinned at Ralph and thanked him for his story of survival. She liked to think that she too could overcome such threats. The girl was so young and yet got herself out of a life and death situation! Maddy hoped her extra-long years pointed toward her own survival. She didn't feel quite so swampy anymore and decided to head west to the Gulf on this humid August day. That Ralph person had probably known what he was talking about. She could hear it in the confident tone of his voice. A certain lifting of his shoulders told her that storms and swamps were important. It made her appreciate today's calm sun.

One day at the end of summer she decided to take a new route to the Gulf. She again came upon Ralph, the native Floridian. So much of life was happenstance. She didn't know why she remembered his name.

"Am I almost to the water?"

"Yup. Another ten minutes maybe. Beautiful waves today, but they can become immense in another month or two."

He seemed not to remember her. His voice sounded like a general greeting to a stranger.

Maddy thought she had better go and appreciate today's view. She again said her goodbye. Ralph looked at her more closely this time, his tan face registering a question. She caught a glimpse of his raised eyebrows, noticed his bristles of interrogation marks. Older men got wise, thicker eyebrows with age. She turned to go. She shouted back at him over her shoulder: "Thanks again for your story about the girl and the alligator!" She saw sudden memory on his face and then headed toward the Gulf.

Maddy thought she had no answers for anyone's questions. She probably would never make a lasting impression on any man. Maybe the Gulf would lure the truth buried in her, allow her to be self-revelatory. And she was right, the sight of the water immersed her in the beauty of the day. The waves roused up motion and told her to walk along the shore. She could gallop like a horse, head upright, nostrils flared in the wind. She slowed her prance. She had better start heading back to her trailer before her legs gave out. She stomped the power of the waves upon her mind.

The days spun by. Suddenly it was hurricane season. A voice on the radio said it was the calm before the storm. She felt moisture gathering in the humid air. When she looked out her window she saw that the renters who owned cars were packing to leave. She walked over to the grocery store to buy supplies. She became even more alarmed when there was no bottled water left on the shelf.

She had no basement to huddle in, as she would have during a tornado in Wisconsin. She knew that tornados could happen anywhere. North or South. Maddy thought of the difference between the two storms: the twisted howl of a train wreck across a city, the fierce hurricane surge of an immense wall of water along the coast. She sat remembering the beauty of her view of the Gulf, the power of the galloping waves.

The voice on the radio warned that Edward was approaching land. She wondered why the weather authorities always named hurricanes after people. Then people who had that name would carry the recollection of destruction around with them. She was glad it wasn't a woman this time. She sat trance-like in her trailer. She felt calm in the back of her eyes. Her arms, legs, torso were building a crescendo of power. Yet the hurricane had the higher power. Maddy knew she could be blown away, eaten alive by swells.

She shook herself out of her trance, grabbed her purse and the remainder of her monthly money. She left to board a Greyhound bus at the nearby transit station. The wind, stronger and stronger, whipped her limbs and hair into a frenzy. She was all akimbo. She struggled forward. The swells were coming. She had no water to drink. The miracle of the Greyhound bus was upon her. It seemed much sturdier than the clickety-clack of a train. People jostled aboard. She was lucky to get a seat. Out the bus window she could see the surging crowd. She thought she saw the question on Ralph's face in her own reflection: "How do I know you?" She remembered Ralph recounting the power of the twelve-year-old girl's defeat of the alligator.

Even the natives were leaving their boarded-up houses. Edward was that strong. The bus pulled out immediately, joined the caravan heading north. The driver said they could pay him at the first inland harbor. The bus stopped in the safe haven of Muscle Shoals, the Alabama town that held the power of music. She gratefully paid the driver and got off at the station. Maddy gave herself the time to tour Fame Studios, where back in the late 1960s the sound began to happen. Fame's walls displayed photos of some artists who inhabited these halls: The Rolling Stones, Etta James. Aretha Franklin, so many more. Muscle Shoals was a turning point in many careers, especially Aretha's. She enjoyed looking at the photos while Aretha belted "Respect" over the speaker system, which oddly seemed to emanate from the bathroom. Later, watching a documentary, she learned that musicians ensconced themselves on and around the john for maximum sound effect.

Maddy returned to the Greyhound station and bought herself a one-way ticket to Wisconsin. When her bus pulled out to head north, she sat back to study her mental picture of the Gulf, a gesture of farewell and a silent "thank you" to that Ralph guy. She had it in the core of her center to be that calm, that strong. She thought again of the girl who saved herself from the alligator, reached inside to find her own strength of purpose. She named herself a hurricane, purged the man who had broken her, swelled up with her new power, and gained strength as the bus sped north. She couldn't wait to feel the rush of cold, cleansing air in her nostrils.

Respect

Maddy walked down the aisle of the Greyhound, past the lady chomping down on a piece of fried chicken. She found herself a window seat toward the back of the bus. The woman had a smile of contentment on her greasy face. Maddy hoped that her decision to return to Wisconsin would get her to that same smiling place of gratified paradise.

The woman held her basket up, turned, and offered her some chicken. "Homemade" was all she said. Maddy smiled and nodded. The stop in the safe haven of Muscle Shoals, Alabama, had involved a lot of walking through the Fame music studio, and the bus station food machines had looked less than appealing. The woman shook her swaying basket down the aisle and sat next to her. Wafts of crisp coating lured Maddy to dig in.

She couldn't help but think of Aretha Franklin. She had just felt the Queen's presence all over the Fame. Her generous vocal demanding "Respect." The Blues Brothers movie where she was a waitress, taking food orders, giving orders. "Think."

The new next-door companion introduced herself as Nettie. Her sturdy brown fingers handed over the basket, Maddy chose a thigh, her favorite part. While she savored the crispy chicken, Nettie filled her in on her travel plans. "Going up north to visit my daughter. Thought I'd cook me up some Southern fried chicken to remember myself by."

They settled in for the long haul and learned more about each other along the way. The hurricane along the Gulf had been horrible, but Nettie lived away from the coast and so missed the brunt of it. Maddy was in the thick of the storm and was glad for the companionship, appreciated the nudge of respect in Nettie's peaceful offering of chicken after the terror of the coastal surge.

Nettie chatted and chomped. She offered Maddy more chicken. Maddy chose another thigh. She liked the dark meat better. The tenderness seemed to make more sense. Nettie confided that her daughter was an excellent cook and would have good food waiting for her. "Our dream is to someday open a little café, call it Paradise Alley." It wasn't only the food; it was about their confidence in each other. Maddy thought: "Will I ever get to that place in life?" She was heading back to Wisconsin with her only friend Eleanor on the horizon. Could she make more? Was she confident enough in her ability to reach out after Stuart had jilted her?

The bus crossed the border into Southern Illinois and Nettie rose to go, swung her Naw-boned chicken basket down the rhythm of the aisle. She turned to smile back at Maddy: "See you in Paradise Alley Café someday!"

Maddy settled in for the last leg of her journey. She got ready to meditate on her survival from the storm. But a disheveled gray-haired gentleman was walking down the aisle toward her. He was wearing a tool belt that was sagging down his pants. He settled in next to her and kept fingering his row of tools, like he was trying to figure out which ones to use to fix a broken world. Maddy thought maybe she could bring him out of himself by speaking: "Yes, I think the world needs fixing too. Wish I was more adept with my hands . . ."

The man looked at her and smiled. "Yup . . . I'm not sure it will be any better in Wisconsin, but I'm going to give it a try. The world doesn't seem to work back home or anywhere else." Maddy tried to show him the respect that Nettie had just given her. "I've been through that recent Edward hurricane and need to get back to Wisconsin. I know things will be better there."

The man sighed and said he was from Indiana. He didn't know if Wisconsin was far enough away. He had found his well-worn tool belt sitting on a folding table at a garage sale his wife had organized. "How could she assume I wouldn't care?" He sighed. He admitted it made him feel the same emptiness he had felt when he went away to college and his parents sold his baseball card collection. Yesterday he snatched up his tool belt from the garage sale table and left. He had thought to go visit his daughter in Bloomington, but she was writing a dissertation on a topic nobody would be interested to read: how the layers of the earth gave off clues to our origins. He looked at Maddy. "Who could possibly wonder about so esoteric a subject?"

Maddy felt she had to defend this daughter. "What she is doing means a great deal to the world. If we find out where we came from we can learn where we are going." She laughed. It seemed a funny thing to say while riding on a bus. People had tickets with the destinations stamped on them. But meaning went beyond any stamp of approval. The man shrugged. He didn't seem so sure.

They crossed the Wisconsin border and Maddy began to gather her things for her stop in Madison. The man's blank stare made her hesitate. He was fingering his pliers like maybe he could put things back together. Or was it to tear things further apart?

"How far north you going?"

"Green Lake. The water is deep. Rough this fall season. Enticing."

Maddy stood, scooted past the man and made her way up to the front of the bus. She put a request in to the driver, handed him the extra money he required for the longer trip. She called Eleanor on her cell phone, told her sorry, she would be delayed.

When the bus pulled in to Green Lake they both got off. It was a small town so they didn't have to walk far to get to the water. The fall wind whipped across the lake. It was its own force, neither hurricane nor tornado. There was a fancy hotel called Heidel House on the lake that rented boats. She was glad when he asked for a rowboat. That seemed safer than a canoe or a kayak or a power boat. The attendant tossed a life preserver into the boat. It landed near a rusty coffee can containing fish hooks and a fillet knife. The man did not put the preserver on. "I'm glad you came along, but now I have to do this alone." She asked if she could hold his tool belt for him. It looked so damn heavy. She was surprised when he agreed.

She sat on a picnic table in the gazebo and stared out into the lake. She could see him maneuver the oars so that he went out. She was afraid for him. Life couldn't be that bad. She had just gone through a hurricane. She had tried to tell him.

Someone from the Heidel House brought her a big soft blanket. See? People can be generous. Like Nettie. We want to respect our origins. His daughter, with her anthropological research, was trying to teach him this. Please let the rough cold water teach him this. She walked down to the shore with the blanket around her shoulders, looking for instruction in indigenous ways. She bent down and fingered the dirt. Her hand caught the shell of a bug that had swum up onto the earth to die. She touched the remains of the delicate creature. This is where it all began. Or was it earlier? Stardust to mud.

The sun made one last stab in the lowering sky. Maddy sat back down in the gazebo. She fingered the shell, looked out over the chomping water in search of its many secrets. She could see the man rowing, churning things up. Suddenly a voice told her to look down. She had been so intent on watching him. Sticking up from a slot on the tool belt was a cell phone. She reached inside her purse for her portable charger, waited, then looked at recent calls. Many were from the same number. She dialed. A frantic woman answered and introduced herself as Melanie, his wife. Maddy explained his trip to Green Lake. She decided not to tell the wife that he was out on the water. What good could the worry do?

"He has been so unpredictable lately. He didn't tell anyone where he was going. I'm getting in my car right now . . . Be there by early morning."

Maddy looked at the lowering sky. The oars were turning, churning up the water. She pulled the blanket closer around her body, a teepee sense of domestic bliss. What she wouldn't give for the companionship of a man. The man in the rowboat was not like the man who had hurt her. The hurricane had helped her purge Stuart, the one who broke her spirit.

She looked out again. The man was rowing back over the rough water. The gazebo must have been his beacon. She would share this generous blanket with him, would respect him, give him his space to work things out. Now was not the time to give anything more than a hand up.

They sat next to each other, the wigwam of the blanket enfolding them. Eyes pierced out into the crisp night sky. She took his hand, felt his pulse. She handed him the bug carcass. He fingered the message of origins. "This carcass makes me think of my daughter's work with the layers of the earth. My arms felt the same in the churning of the water, told me to get back to shore." He took out a crumpled white handkerchief and gently folded it around the carcass, put the delicate message into his shirt pocket. The cloth seemed damp. Had he been anointed by Green Lake? Or had he cried before even getting on the bus? Maddy hoped that one body spoke to the other body. Something was being born. They sat in the harbor of deep water. In the morning Melanie would be here to take him home.

Easy To Be Hard

Eleanor's daughter Alice came home from a high school history class asking about Leo Burt, the campus bomber who was never caught. The kids thought of him as a mystery man. Eleanor had her own theory. She had been on the University of Wisconsin-Madison campus in 1970 at the time of the Sterling Hall bombing and knew of Leo Burt, although she didn't know him personally.

"He was a quiet guy, physically strong enough to be on the crew team. Into writing and meditation. No one guessed he could kill."

Alice looked at her quizzically.

"But they didn't mean to kill anyone, just mess up the army military stuff."

"True. But I think he felt so bad about that man's death he just couldn't live with himself." Eleanor shivered with the memories of those difficult years. She went back inside her mind.

She told Alice how as a young woman beginning grad school she had taken the bus down to Madison from Ripon, the purported birthplace of the Republican Party, to look for an apartment. In high school she had heeded the nuns' warnings about "the pagan institute" in the state capital and gone to Ripon, a small local private college. But then she had been accepted into graduate school at the big university. She was tired of the veils at church, the white gloves worn to

Sunday brunch, and the 10:00 pm curfews. The apartment needed to be somewhere near the vast campus. She didn't have much money, so she would need to live with strangers. After a long day of looking, she decided on a small room in a little white house kitty-corner from the zoo. Her two roommates turned out to be serious students and they pretty much went their own way.

The sounds from the zoo were her first friends. Every day at 4:00 pm the lions were guttural in anticipation of food. The lonely human-raised wolf voiced his longing. She went across the street to try to soothe him, but the cage kept them distant. She knew enough about the law not to cross the line. A woman had been detained and fined for petting the nose of a giraffe.

She could walk up to her English classes in about forty minutes. She loved words and flew through the assigned books. In just a year of work and walks and zoo companionship she was ready to take her master's exam.

On a Saturday in May she trudged up Bascom Hill past the statue of Abraham Lincoln, touching his big foot for courage and fortitude. The foot reminded her of the original inhabitants walking this land, building the Native American effigy mounds the white males would displace with concrete in Bascom Hall's construction. Imagine her surprise when she was met at the entrance of the building by armed National Guard members. She hadn't been involved in the student protests or Dow Chemical's creation of murderous napalm. The anti-Vietnam movement had begun without her participation. But now here were these stern men. They stood shoulder to shoulder, hardened, hands on their weapons, demanding to see her student ID card before they would allow her to enter the building. She didn't even know if she had it with her! She started pawing through her purse and finally found the identification card and handed it over. Her photo showed a smiling, anticipating face. She was frowning now. The guards let her in.

The room was filled with about forty nervous people. The crowd didn't surprise her. Eleanor had been raised at a time when people thought they could still get tenure jobs teaching in the Humanities, a time before those jobs became grains of sand blowing off a piece of broken driftwood. As she paged through the long list of questions, she saw that the exam was structured to show a wide range of knowledge: everything from *Beowulf* to Vonnegut. The armed guards had startled her into acute awareness. The effigy mounds came alive in her mind and she used the energy of winged birds to resurrect interior thoughts. She crafted her word flights on the blue book pages.

On her walk home she looked down to try to steady her exhilaration. She knew she had done well on the exam. And there, etched into the sidewalk when it had been still wet, precisely written with either a sharp twig or a chisel were the words "easy to be hard." It was from a Three Dog Night song currently playing on Radio Free Madison. She smiled as she climbed the stairs to her small room.

Just before sleep she thought about that song . . . how Three Dog Night moved from the carefree "Joy to the World" to the hard lament "How can people be so heartless?" Something in the guardsmen's faces created in her a new consternation.

The next day she tried to soothe herself with a walk to Memorial Library. There were more students than usual on University Avenue; they were all heading toward Library Mall. Up ahead, she heard voices through microphones. She saw a woman tie a bandana on her face, covering her mouth and nose. A half block from Library Mall students started running and yelling. She was caught up in the crowd and began running with them. She felt the pulse of their anger at how wrong the war was. She thought about the obtrusive stance of the National Guardsmen yesterday. Their hardened faces. And their guns.

Suddenly the air grabbed her by the throat. Tear gas was in her lungs. Her eyes teared over in absolute sorrow. She trekked her trail of tears back toward her apartment, gasping for breath and rubbing her eyes. She gradually regained her normal breathing and steadied herself on the walk home. Eleanor remembered coming again to the words on the sidewalk, realizing she had read them both upside down and right side up, and knowing she would join the throb of anger for the rest of her days on campus. It wasn't all about books. That night she saw her discontented face on the local news.

The month of May was a turning point for her campus activism. When the National Guardsmen killed four students at Kent State she was horrified but not surprised. There was a front page photo in *The Capital Times* of a young woman raising her hands in the air asking "Why?" She knelt in anguish next to a young dead student on the grounds of Kent State. The photo brought the war home. The dead young people were on the ground, in the cement. Her generation's music had gone from carefree, to sorrowful, to angry. That summer the war protesters heard the drumming, "four dead in Ohio." Rock and roll music had the insistent beat of Native American spirits reclaiming their burial mounds. Madison was in the same state of turmoil as Ohio. The Sterling Hall bombing happened later that same summer. By then she had been reading Leo Burt's column in *The Daily Cardinal*. She had felt violated by tear gas more than once.

Eleanor watched Alice take all these personal memories to heart.

"Holy wizardry, Mom. You were so involved. People saw you protesting on the local news. You made a statement!"

The high school students were continuing the discussion of the Vietnam era in their history class. One day Alice came home extra excited. They had watched a documentary on the student protests. She proudly told Eleanor what she said to the class: "That's my mother, up there on the screen, etched into the film."

Eleanor thought again about Leo Burt. There were no images of him left. It felt as if his face had blown up in the cement of the army math research center. Yet here she was, moving through the documented history of the film, drumming her discontent.

Magic Carpet Ride

Eleanor had taken Peter on board when he was seven, trying to win him over by reading him rollicking passages from *Huckleberry Finn*. Then she followed Huck's example and went fishing along the Yahara River with Peter, this new boy in her life, the wired child of her husband Ray's first scary foray into marriage. The boy showed no patience for fishing. Ray demonstrated to his fidgety son how to hold a steady line. Eleanor realized in his calm hand he held the secret to a good life. She could tell a lot about a person from how they treated their kids. She loved Ray for his attention to his son. In due time he would be just as patient with their daughter Alice.

She blinked in the insistence of sunlight on the river and time ran away. Ray was ill for a long time and then died, way too young, when Alice was in middle school. Eleanor reeled with numbness during and after the funeral. She tried to help Alice through the loss, the whole time crying out for solitude. She wanted to be alone with her memories. But she was busy with PTA during the high school years. When Alice moved away for college the widow in her began to realize that solitude only caused more grief.

She tried reaching out to others. Enrichment classes. Water aerobics. She started going to a little neighborhood place called Atlas Café where the waitresses called her "honey" and even once in a while "darlin.'" She went often just to hear their women-of-the-world voices. The coffee was hot and the food was good. Since she was alone she at first tried to sit at a small side table, but most days the only chairs available were at a long communal table in the middle of the room. Soon she was a member of the breakfast regulars, Food for Thought they called themselves, mostly retired folks who came for the food and the waitresses and, after a while, each other's company.

She noticed the brasher ones first, the old geezer with bushy eyebrows proud to announce that his ex-wife paid him alimony just to be rid of him. He was good for her first laugh of the day. The footloose and fancy-free bleached blonde was on the prowl for an interesting man. She assured the men in their little group that they were safe from her clutches. The married couple proved that even people who'd been together a long time could communicate in the give and take of conversation. Other than herself there was one more widow still trying to come to terms with her new world. She sighed a lot but seemed to appreciate the camaraderie. Finally, the quiet poet pulled his chair up to the head of the table and treated them to thoughts sparsely spoken out loud: "chew the sweet rain," "take me away on a flying carpet." He brought magic into their day.

These people gave her renewed courage to try and reach out to Peter. He had never really warmed up to her over-reaching attempts at love, her swim down the Yahara pulling the rubber raft holding father and son. Peter was now on his own, a young adult with a job and a girlfriend. Eleanor wanted to commiserate about their loved one gone to that great casting of stars in the sky. From the moment he picked up the phone she could hear the raging war in his voice. "Don't call me. I don't want to have anything to do with you." He slammed down his phone. She hung up and, in frustration, punched her fist into the wall. She had never felt so misunderstood and unloved in her entire life. Why was Peter being so cruel? The hand hurt like hell. Peter used disdain to try to torture her. Her own personal civil war was erupting and Peter ran away from his step-mother and his half-sister Alice's range of sight. She had the throbbing wound on her fist as a constant reminder.

Eleanor sat in her only chair, looked at the crack in the wall, the loose plaster where her hand had hit. Her little dog Spud knew something was wrong and jumped into her lap to offer comfort. Holding Spud, looking into his pleading eyes, made her start to see how the rift may have begun. Her step-son must have gotten greed into his head. He thought she owed him money for selling the house she and Ray owned together. After the funeral she and Alice had moved into a small apartment. The house sat on the market a long time, then had to be let go in a short sale. Add to that the threatening pile-up of medical bills from her battle to keep an ill man alive and her bottom line was very little to live on. Peter withheld sympathy for her plight. Silence was his weapon of choice. In her heart she knew that to be shunned was a grave punishment.

Her right hand ricocheted with pain. The doctor informed her that she had broken a bone in her right index finger. She was right-handed! She would need to hunker down and heal. Meanwhile the finger was wound with gauze and plastered. At least it wasn't her middle finger stuck up to say "screw the world" for the months it would take to mend. Instead it was a finger that appeared to be pointing in a direction.

The Food for Thought friends were curious about her newly bandaged finger. The geezer said "move on, no one is worth the pain." Fancy Free said to call him again, that things have a way of working themselves out. The married couple sipped their coffee and pondered his motivations: Insecurity? The pressure of being a young man in love? Anger pounding in his genes? The influence of his birth mother? "Dig deeper." The widow sighed, "live for yourself, not for him." Eleanor listened intently. The more they conjured up reasons the dearer these friends became. Funny how empathetic words could calm a worried mind. Maybe Peter's motivations were more complicated than mere greed. Then the quiet poet had the final say. He looked up from his plate of sunny side eggs and crisp bacon: "You can't make a person be who they are not." He handed Eleanor some bacon for Spud. As he passed his plate closer she could see that the eggs were bright eyes opening her world. Chew rain. Chew on possibility. The poet's smile was detonating her arsenal of pain. A rough-voiced waitress boxed the bacon up for her.

On her walk home she went over the Food for Thought advice in her mind. A gentle rain dampened her thoughts. It started raining harder, cleansing away the vestiges of war. She opened her apartment door and shook her hair like a dog to get it dry. Spud greeted her with his stub tail wagging.

"I love you! I smell bacon! Did you bring me bacon?"

Eleanor held Spud close, was in tune with his joyful beating heart. She put him down on his little carpet bed, grabbed the treat with her left hand, then made him sit for his bacon. She felt his lick of a kiss on her leg. She knew disarming solace in his gratitude. The quiet poet's smile flew in front of her. He had given her the gift of words. She sat in her chair, lay her heart down like a carpet, a scruff of love to be woven into friendship, or stomped on, or knelt on, or spirited away from a wound to a healing place.

Light the Dark

Maddy stepped off the bus in Madison with a sense of relief. She had survived a hurricane in Florida and a bus trip across the country. Her friend Eleanor's bright face was at the station, ready to drive her to her new apartment. Eleanor had arranged for the new place. It was what a friend does. She had learned all about it on her bus trip, about accepting gifts and lending a helping hand. Basic life lessons: accept with gratitude a piece of chicken, save a drowning man. How life wasn't just about herself.

The apartment was in an older building near Breese Stevens Field. A welcoming front porch added to the charm. She would be around lots of people. Eleanor had stocked the refrigerator to get her started. They sat in her new apartment drinking tea. Maddy cupped her hands around the warm mug. The tea baptized her throat. Maddy had gone nearly insane when Stuart left her. She remembered her reaction to Stuart's departure: to invent crazy lyrics and sing loudly at Café Zumba. Eleanor, who had tried to rescue her from the raging lyrics, sat smiling at her. "New songs, happier songs, will come out." She left to return to her own nearby place. "I'll be back to listen to your journey."

Maddy sat on the glider on her front porch. How Midwest! No gated turn away places here. In Florida people turned their backs to the wall. The poster on the telephone pole outside her porch announced today's final event of the Breese season: a convocation of food carts to celebrate their successful spring, summer, and fall. Judges would be present to announce who would be awarded prime locations next spring.

She decided to stroll over to the old open-air stadium, scene of many baseball games, soccer matches, frisbee throws, and music over the years. The gates opened upon a field of food carts. The grass still had a summer "give" to it, still soft enough to stand and sit on. Open views, not a bad seat in the bleachers. People jostled in a friendly way. The mood swung with a festival of spices and music filled the air. The longest lines were in front of Mexican and Thai carts, but Maddy chose to go for a humble Italian offering. She just about choked on her spaghetti when she saw Stuart in the line for Thai. Should she go up to him when he had left her so abruptly? She revisited that sabotaged feeling. She was in shock. She'd thought he was out of the country on one of his treasure hunts. Up ahead Lynette and Virginia Rose were strumming guitars. Voices sent the message, Lynette's low and growly, Virginia Rose's high and pure and their power permeated the air. Maddy thought of her stop in Muscle Shoals, how Aretha Franklin's vocal range dominated the music studio.

Children gathered around the local singers, learning the meaning of being strong. Maddy sat with them to finish her spaghetti. When she looked back up Stuart had disappeared into the crowd. Just as well.

Maddy wandered through the stadium. All the food carts were running out of goods. It was time to say goodbye for the season. Lynette and Virginia Rose were still into their gig. They began that old Neil Young classic "Like a Hurricane." Their combined sounds sent a gust through Maddy.

A hurricane can be named for a man or a woman. She had been in Florida, had literally just been through the swells. It had been a man this time. And then she saw Stuart coming toward her. When he brushed by her on his way out she felt his body, the departure of his power. She did not hesitate: "Hello. Goodbye." Sardonic. She hoped he was intelligent enough to read her tone.

He looked at her like a pirate wanting to jump ship. "Hi. Sailing for Spain soon."

She thought of Dylan's lyrics for "Boots of Spanish Leather." His words had helped her survive her initial craziness. She felt a delicious tingle of relinquishment as she watched Stuart walk away. It was then Maddy knew that music would continue to see her through these inevitable storms. In the days ahead she would sit on her front porch and tell Eleanor all about it. Now was the time to invent her own lyrics. On her way out the Breese Stevens gate she sang: "Swell the earth/look deep and high/you'll find me on the other side." The other side could be the moon. Or a relationship. Or the result of evolution as found in looking at the layers of the earth. Planetary energy. Light after a hurricane.

Maddy sat back down in her front porch glider, rocking back and forth with recent memories. Her mind spoke to Eleanor. Can't wait to see you. Here's the influence for my new lyrics. A strong pump up: Goodbye Stuart. Hello new words. Goodbye hurricane. Hello cleansing air. Goodbye upheaval. Hello generous cross-country bus ride. Pause. Her legs went back under. Goodbye threat of drowning. Hello hand, a life preserver across the water. She got her feet back on the ground. Hello all who crawl upon this earth. Hello filtering stardust light.

Urgent

Amy wanted to be normal, to get up in the morning and go to exercise class and then have a productive day. She understood the little enclave she had created: The old house in the safe neighborhood and the computer class that would connect her to the larger world she had lost when she lost her husband. But something was keeping her up at night, some tug at the heart that pulled her up, not down.

Winged thoughts flew through her. She began to write. Maybe it was a goodbye letter. At his funeral she had placed George's beloved hat on his chest. Then they closed the casket and darkness descended. She requested that he be cremated, and that his hat be there to comfort him. When she scattered his ashes over his favorite fishing spot some lifted in the wind, a bird in flight. She kept hearing about all the spouses who left that way, instead of just decaying in a hole in the ground. Other women's voices told her that flying was preferable. Those widowed voices kept her awake. 3:00 am and she was in a fermentation process: effervescent language danced upon the page. Mead. Bottom's up. That Puckish Shakespeare imp sprung to life.

Her little seventeen-year-old dog Orbit still had that playfulness. Now he lay in his comforting round bed, sides curled up around him. She was wide awake when he was smart enough to know when to rest. She was trying to prepare for a normal day. Amy knew she needed to pick up his animal message. She appreciated every day she had with him.

She managed to get some sleep. The alarm was set for 7:00 am so she could get to exercise class and then to work at the Pharmacy School. She was grateful to get out of the house and explore the world. Amy took on the role of Standardized Patient, pretending to pick up prescriptions with prospective Pharmacy School graduates. They needed practical experience on how to provide medication consultation. Her job was to be dramatic, to evoke different scenarios as a problem client. They videotaped her and the students learned from the interactions. The challenge was to invent different personalities and be convincing. Amy could put the pharmacy students through several cantankerous or scattered or fumbling situations. At times she was picking up diabetic medicine while chewing on a candy bar. Sometimes she was angry at being told to swallow so much stuff. Sometimes she was double-parked and her new blood pressure cuff showed her off the charts. She had it within herself to be that temperamental. It was fun, taking on the careless role or non-functional role or angry role or the hurried role or the lost role. It was hard too because she had to park in the same lot of the same hospital where George had died. Urgent. Emergency. Corridors of virus. Maybe she needed to face the loss head on so she could move on.

Amy went to exercise class, came home to shower. She needed to leave for work. Her hand was still on the inside front door knob when she suddenly heard the crashing of glass. Closing the door, she went upstairs to investigate. There was a huge wild bird swooping around in her bathroom! No wing broken. No blood. She closed the door.

She thought immediately to crate Orbit so he would not be devoured.

Her first call was to the Humane Society, but she only got a recording. Then she called Madison Animal Services and got through. With the wild bird still flapping around upstairs, she called the Pharmacy School and explained why she would not be in. A wild bird. Could they understand? The voice on the other end sounded incredulous.

She went outside the house just to feel safer and waited for Animal Control. The guy came within a half-hour, wearing thick long gloves and carrying a huge crate. He looked up, saw the gaping hole in her bathroom window, and guessed the rest.

She had to wait and wonder for an agonizingly long twenty minutes before he came out with the bird in the crate and said she was smart to get out, to crate her dog. It was a young red-tailed hawk, just learning to hunt. She could see the sharp talons struggling through the bars on the crate when he was carried away. The hawk's eyes fixated on some distant point in the sky. The man promised the bird would be released into a safe place away from houses.

The Communication Arts professor who taught the Pharmacy School course about medicine consultation called her into her office. She wanted to know why Amy had missed her appointment with the students. After all, interviews with Standardized Patients were an important part of the learning process they needed to graduate.

Amy took on her most charming persona and explained about the wild bird, about how it was a once in a lifetime experience. Like a proud retriever she deposited the image of the hawk to the professor. Her mouth felt a piercing from holding the image. The bird was a reality flying against the walls of her bathroom. The professor could check the facts. Animal Control would have a record. How do you prepare for urgency within the reverberation of your own home? She promised to be in the video station from now on. The professor studied her face, then praised her convincing work with the students and kept her on. Amy shivered with the knowledge that she would park near the "Urgent" sign in the hospital parking lot every time she put on her actress persona. What she didn't say to the professor or to anyone else except herself was the urgency of how she really felt. About how the hawk had lifted away her husband's ashes when she had scattered them, how the powerful bird had returned him to her and then released him back into the wild, how life arrived with tumultuous force and carried her forward.

If Dogs Run Free

The little mutt was standing outside in front of Eleanor's living room window, gazing at her in the freezing November rain. She glanced over at Charles, but he had his head buried in the newspaper, as usual. Eleanor looked back at the shivering dog. She couldn't tell where the rain stopped and the dog's tears began. Her voice brought Charles back to their real-life situation. While Charles said he didn't want the responsibility of ownership, Eleanor pleaded her case. "Look at that quivering drenched coat." Charles rolled his eyes and relented. They opened the door and the mongrel shook the wet from his coat, a baptism of gratitude.

The small terrier-like mutt fit right in with their family. They no longer had to worry about cleaning up morsels of food. They named him Frank because he was honest about his affections, then added an "ie" for endearment. She made Frankie a main character in the story on her refrigerator door, an open page from her diary. She put up a picture of Frankie chewing on a pinecone like he was savoring a celebratory cigar. Also up on the refrigerator door were Eleanor's happy family photos, her ninety-two-year-old mother blowing out the candles on her birthday cake, her brood of offspring smiling around her. Eleanor's daughter Alice's proud college graduation. Under the magnet proclaiming "Eat at Smiley's and Get Gas," a grocery list. Up on top, on the freezer door, a Fire and Rescue magnet placed just in front of the vial stored in the freezer with a medication list. At the very top, held by a magnet of horses running along the beach, manes and tails merging with the waves, was what Eleanor considered to be the best poem she had ever written, titled "Carvings," about how the landscape changed forever after a tornado. Next to that was a motto she tried to live by, held on by a magnetic swallow Alice had recently sent her from Capistrano: "My goal is to someday be the person my dog thinks I am."

Charles had nothing to add to the display on the refrigerator. When she had first met him seven years after her first husband's death, they had naturally hit it off, laughing and walking the countryside. Now he was becoming a closed book. She tried to understand him. As a concession to Charles, she hired a young college woman as a dog walker so he wouldn't be bothered with the task when she was away looking for work.

The next few years passed and Charles began to be even more distant. She went to Frankie for solace. The problem was that her husband stopped looking for the poetry that held strong residence in her heart. Frankie could find her depths just by being near. Eleanor named Frankie chief caretaker of the household. She felt she had to go on an archeological dig to uncover her buried words and so deferred everyday caregiving to her beloved dog. Sure, she had established herself as alpha from the beginning. Dogs liked to know where they stood in the pack. Frankie was all about admiration. He could be in the next room and still know what she was thinking. Dogs could detect moods and cancer. They could tell if you were slipping into an unlit space and use a wet nose to bring you back. He loved her for telling him where he stood. People needed to know where they stood too. Charles was not equipped to understand her. Instinct told her to find someone stronger. Then he proved her right by running away with that young flirtatious dog walker.

There were separation papers to sign. Luckily, her brother was a lawyer. Save for the embarrassment of acknowledging a failed relationship, she wouldn't have to pay much. Eleanor found a job shelving books at the library in the little town just down the road, liked being close to all those interesting titles. She hoped to be able to keep the house. She devoted the rest of her time to Frankie. He would come up to her with his eyes pleading for a free run. Together they would explore the miles of surrounding trails. One trail led to a small pond where she would skip stones and Frankie would dive in. She started swimming too, remembering from her girlhood days at camp that you should have a water buddy. She felt safer with Frankie than she ever had with Charles. Skip stones. Skip out. Skip a beat.

She decided to get out of the house more and began volunteering at the local Humane Society. The people in charge wanted to make the dogs as adoptable as possible. That was the reason they gave for not allowing the volunteers to bring along their own dogs. Pay attention to the task at hand. The lonely dogs were so appreciative. They made themselves naturally available. When she returned home from these excursions Frankie exhibited marvelous behavior, more curious than jealous. His nose picked up the whole story.

Eleanor and Frankie still spent a lot of time together. One June day they were sitting in the backyard. The geese had been populous and they left messes everywhere. The television repairman remarked on their presence and called them "Canadian carp." Frankie always knew just what to do: he ran barking at the geese and off they flew. Eleanor watched Frankie do the good work of chasing off the geese, hummed the scat background of Maeretha Stewart on Bob Dylan's "If Dogs Run Free." She liked it when Dylan relied on a woman's voice.

By mid-summer the geese had gotten the message and landed on the other side of the vast trails. She celebrated her willingness to allow Frankie his freedom. Then how to explain his attitude toward the crane family who visited their yard, gracefully keeping their distance, showing off their youngster? Frankie remained quietly at her feet. As summer progressed the cranes edged closer and closer until she could see the red circle highlighting their eyes. They were showing off their young ones. The dog respected the cranes' sanctified place in her heart. Eleanor thanked Frankie for his perception, gave him extra head scratches.

She found an interesting book in the animal behavior section of the library that said a dog is happiest when he has work to do. In that same section of the library the staff had hung a print by the abstract artist Joan Mitchell: "George went Swimming at Barnes Hole, But It Got Too Cold." Eleanor looked intently at the print for many days. The subject was a standard bred black poodle with a water-resistant coat. In the print yellows turned to whites. Waves were caught up in the tangled brush strokes, a patch of grays and blues. George the black poodle had run free into the water, was disappearing, getting too cold to move. The winter sky looked down over the dog. Would he go into shock? Joan Mitchell saved George, created a rock for him to stand on, melded ferocity and tranquility in her rescue. Grays and blues turned out to be the saving colors. He became free from the confines of any one brush stroke.

Eleanor felt a power gathering in her own art. Her poetry handed Frankie the job of guardian. She had no one answer, only a surge of fierce words. The absence of Charles gave Frankie another job. He was the force who kept her life in order. New goal: try to act more like your dog. Intuitively. She saddled Frankie with her messages. His saddle contained the jagged fragments of her heart and he happily carried his work forward.

Ring Those Bells

The church bells up the street told Eleanor and Amy that Mass was about to begin. Neither of them believed the calling because it was a programmed chime, not the reverberated clanging of real bells. But the sound was a good way to tell them it was time for the local author reading at the nearby library. You never knew where you might find inspiration.

The days were starting to get longer and there was so much to do. Plant. Weed. Grow. A few clouds added interest to the sky. The grass glistened on their walk. The daffodils were particularly yellow this year. They reached the library and claimed good seats.

Eleanor spied a woman she had met months ago at the neighborhood coffee shop. The woman had been alone, singing a sad song loudly about a guy who had jilted her for a younger woman. When she sang the name "St-u-art" it sounded like an aggrieved howl at the moon. Eleanor worried about her. Loneliness can unhinge us.

"Amy, I see someone I want to say hi to. Save my seat." She would reintroduce herself and see how the woman was doing.

"Hi. Remember me from Café Zumba? I'm Eleanor. How are you?"

"Oh. Hi." Her voice smoothed over the past rough edges. "I'm Maddy. I'm doing much better. Jilted but crawling out of it. Still singing my words but they are softer. Thought I'd get inspiration from these writers."

"Maybe we can meet up after the readings? I'm third row, front and center." They smiled at each other and set the plan in motion.

The crowd hushed and the readings began. A tall strong woman stood and spoke poetry of a conspired childhood and the wonders of motherhood. The poet exposed the pain of living with a father who made it his business to hurt the family. She stood in front of the rapt audience and explored the origins of words. Listeners heard the practical solace of finding words on an archaeological dig. Eleanor and Amy couldn't help but notice her two young daughters wriggling with pride in front of them. Young enough to want to bolt the place but old enough to start appreciating their mother's art. Eleanor imagined their family refrigerator embossed with crayon wonders. The poet's friend or lover bent over to attend to the girls. Eleanor looked back to see Maddy's reaction to the lyrics. Her new friend looked entranced.

Next a guy got up to read some flash fiction. He was casual in a motorcycle jacket, a bulwark against his depth of seeing. The stories sounded close to poetry because the sky and mud were important to him. Red clay and humid air made words cling against the throat. Eleanor held on to each image. His was the age-old story of tarnished knights on a quest. Some of the characters were desperate, others honored a tool belt, a car, a motorcycle. Each one wandered down highways and alleyways to search for thrills and love. Eleanor came to realize that this was a writer who was vulnerable to experience, who admitted his characters could be hurt. She had forgotten that men could be like that. Her first husband had been that vulnerable, but she had lost him so young. Her exes, Charles, and the others she knew would come along didn't care, would up and leave her flat.

The librarian asked the audience if there were questions for the first two readers. Eleanor thought the words spoke for themselves. She used the time to make a meditation on the damage done by the men in her life. Charles was the most hurtful. He gave up trying, even gave up on their sweet dog. She knew he wasn't strong enough for a comeback. Other men would pretend and lie.

She sat in the pale-yellow library room and decided she would figure out why she always chose the wrong man. It probably went back to her father. Like several poets she knew she had a father who put himself in absolute control of the family. Big hurtful black shoes. Heil. She would no longer try to right that wrong. She had been adrift in a current of unforeseen forces. Now she would stop looking for resolution in every man she met. The new knowledge gave her a surge of purification. Her mind came back into the room. From the two readers she had learned there was poetry in etymology and there was quest in sky and mud.

Next a woman stood and spoke a story and played the viola. The music was the best part, necessary to the meaning of the words. She was a bit shy and hesitant, but that was okay. Eleanor could see herself standing there. She closed her eyes and allowed the music to cast a spell.

The audience comments for the third reader were all in praise of her music. The two women whispered, decided to forego the usual swamping of the writers after an event. Eleanor nudged Amy toward the door and introduced her to Maddy. She made a quick decision to say nothing about her concerns. She wanted to see if Maddy could right her own ship.

The three women left the reading together. All agreed it had been an inspirational experience. Eleanor staked out her ground with important words: Motherhood. Cleansing. Sounds. Quest. Promise. Amy's raised fist expressed a surge of radical belief. Maddy's eyes glistened.

They walked the Lake Monona path. Kayaks bobbed and moved forward under the deepening sky. An early half-moon punctuated their thoughts. Eleanor saw the yellow glow as the beginning of a parenthesis, the straight line suggested an exclamation, and the parenthesis of a full moon closure was far off in the distance. All was a possibility. A congress of birds perched in every tree, throats trilling a choral dissonance.

Maddy sang with the birds. "All art is embryos. Love begins with a seed and blooms, bluebells blowing in the breeze, sounding origins. I am born."

Eleanor saw her righted ship as a troubadour for renewal.

Let Maddy's Stuart and the other restless men travel the world. Let them disappear, wrapped in the cloak of flirtatious hair, buried in the wealth of stolen treasure chests. The bluebell flowers rang the truth of the story, the talent emerging right here in this place on earth. Maddy's voice had quivered, shot an arrow to the heart of the matter.

The three women hooked arms and continued down the lake path. Waves touched the shore and anointed mud crea-tures. Eleanor heard Maddy demonstrate her new bravery.

"Did you see the spot on the local news about Wisconsin scientists making a breakthrough in the search for stronger antibiotics? They are studying the emerging insect world. Nature has handed us our answers."

Eleanor and Amy rang in with their agreement. Elea-nor couldn't help but articulate Maddy's observation. "Yes, no synthetics needed. The answer is in nature if we only protect, only look." Amy pointed to the left. "Earthworms farm the Native American Bear Mound, teach us how to make the underground breathe."Their voices hung upright in the branches of every tree. The women felt evolution in the air. That punctuation of a half-moon illuminated the moving waters.

The Laundry Room

Management gave their low-income senior housing building a new washer and dryer. The machines were bigger than the old ones. Louise was glad because now maybe she could wash the old comforter she wrapped around her body every night.

She knew not to do laundry on a Monday, the traditional day where everyone had been trained for years to do it. Her brief stint as a waitress at New Orleans Take Out told her that even in Wisconsin the Monday Special was always red beans and rice. She vaporized herself, determined to break the chains of habit. She experimented with the timing. The new washer took thirty-five minutes, the dryer one hour. Always set it on high. Daytime was not so good. She knew the old ladies nodded off after dinner.

On a Saturday, just after the local evening news, she pushed her load of laundry in the grocery cart from her third-floor apartment down to a lower wing of the building. She liked that the building hugged the earth. The skylight above the machines told her pink was in her future.

A sign said use an energy efficient detergent. All she had was the Free and Clear Purex bought on sale up the street at Walgreens. Perfume gave her a headache.

She decided she better stay and watch the machines, make sure she wasn't destroying these mechanical wonders. Was her comforter too big? Would the washer overflow? Would cascades of sudsy water seep into the hallway? Maybe her sweatshirt would balance the load. She had already been written up by management because she played her radio too loud. One more reprimand and she would be out, back onto the streets.

Louise listened to the chug of the washer doing the vibration of cleaning. It was that new front loading kind so she could see her comforter and hooded sweatshirt turning into each other. There was no overflow, even with the load and the cheap detergent. She noticed for the future so she wouldn't have to stay in the laundry room for the duration of the cycle.

It was time for the dryer. She shoved her two items in and set the knob to high. In went the rest of her quarters. She sat back down to listen to the rhythm of the zipper clicking against the metal drum. She could hear the banging of the toddler shoe she kept from a former life. She still found use for it in the dryer to fluff up feathered items.

Louise heard a shopping cart coming down the hallway. She peered out to see who it was, hoping it was not one of the gossip-mongers. She had chosen to live up on three so she could stay out of the gossip. It was that new resident who moved into the ground floor. She had met this guy at their backyard picnic table. He seemed to like the same old rock and roll music. Her battered radio was her lifeline.

"Hey. Remember me? I'm Rip. We took that walk along the path to the pond."

During their first walk he had explained that his parents were commune people who wanted to tear away from society. Thus the name Rip. When he moved to find his own life he discovered an actor named Rip Torn but he knew that must be a stage name, so he gave himself that name. She thought it suited him, even if he had probably never worn a suit in his life. She was beginning to like everything about him. Her mind went a little crazy and she imagined herself a heroine in a romance novel, him ripping away at her bodice.

Now in the laundry room her mind moved fast. "The dryer's about half done so you should have time to start the washer before someone else gets here."

"Isn't life all about timing?"

She went back to the zipper and shoe beating out a tune. Life was getting a little too dangerous.

"You know, think I'll go up to my apartment until this is done. Free you to get your laundry accomplished."

She came down later to fold her two items. Rip was waiting to put his stuff in the dryer. She noticed lots of underwear and plaid shirts.

Later that night she heard a gentle knock on her door. Rip stood in front of her with his shopping cart full of folded clothes. He left the cart in the hall and brought his laundry basket inside. He touched the backside of his hand to her face, just like he had done at the end of their first walk together. The gesture made Louise shiver and she zippered up her newly clean sweatshirt. His laundry basket spilled over and they both bent down to pick up his shirts and underwear. Their clothes got jumbled together, his plaids and her zipper. The zipper slid down easily. Then they were on the bed, the comforter bunched under them.

Louise felt as if she was in control. Her girlfriends said it was like the chug of a train but she never did like that way of thinking. Rock had always given her the answer. Rolling in the deep. They both hummed several Mick Jagger tunes.

Rambler

Eleanor sat cross-legged on a rock overlooking the community of weavers, imagining she was a Native American squaw. She wanted to hold the pose even though every inch of her old legs ached. She felt all the usual contradictions. How could she be a squaw when white people of yore brought pestilence? Disease reminded her of her disastrous marriage to Charles. A genuine Native American man with dark braids and high cheekbones gazed at her and frowned, the lines on his cheeks deepening with disapproval. His whole stance said she had no business appropriating his peoples' pride or gestures. His presence made her remember that back home the city council had omitted "Squaw Bay" from the map because it was a derogatory way of looking at Native American women. She had been stupid, as usual, and the indigenous man had let her know it.

Eleanor nodded at the man. She knew he was right. She was a quite helpless lost woman. She had picked up with Travis after the disaster of her marriage to Charles. Now Travis had left her in Arizona. He would just explode every time she beat him at cards. It was supposed to be a good climate for asthma, but she felt unable to breathe. The explosions were bad enough, and then came the huffed silence. How they each used silence at the wrong time. It was like Charles all over again. They did fine rambling on about what to do and where to go, but when it came time to say what was in each heart the words got stuck in the throat. After a time this wears a person out. There wasn't anything to be done about it. They were both set in their ways. He had already hopped a Greyhound Bus back to the Midwest, leaving her with her dilapidated Nash Rambler. Maybe she should at least be a tourist with a camera and binoculars. The stereotype. After that cross-legged sitting she limped to her car. The rusty door creaked open and she was on her way.

They had talked about Bryce Canyon National Park. The guidebook said it was a fantasy land, full of colorful limestone etchings. She decided to make southern Utah her destination. The road stretched out before her with a vibration of desolation. She couldn't imagine what was supposed to be so great about it. Southern Utah seemed just as bleak as Arizona.

There was a tourist bus parked, blocking the view. She got in line with the other tourists for Bryce Canyon. It involved considerable walking but she had the right shoes for it. And every step was worth the effort: a marvel of wind sculpted design. Eleanor felt the worshipful spirit of Navajo people in the bridge the wind had built for them. They walked over the natural quiet of eons of wind and water carvings. She was with the people without trying to emulate them. The spirit of that frowning Native man appeared, voicing his approval. She began dream drumming, reaching out for the spirits that lived in the ever-changing formations. She had read that even today some indigenous people didn't want to have their photograph taken because they were afraid they'd disappear. Why use binoculars when the Spirit Bird will come to you? Bryce Canyon spoke to her and told her she was doing exactly what she needed to do.

The park guide stood in front of them and said that the Native American words for Bryce Canyon (named for a Mormon architect) mean "red rocks standing like men in a bowl-shaped canyon." The Native American words seemed more fitting for the landscape than the last name of a visiting Mormon. The Native words reached out to her and told her that she was not lonely. That just because you are alone doesn't mean you have to be lonely. She was standing with all the people who came before. Then she was floating apart from the tourist crowd and became one with the Wind and Bird Spirits who guided her thoughts. The fantasy red rocks had been worth the journey. She got into her creaking old Rambler and let out a sigh, determined to keep this place in her thoughts.

Before heading west she stopped at another trading post and bought a blanket from a weathered Navajo woman. She saw the years of experience in her gnarled hands. The woman showed her the geometric diamond patterns, the white pony for the Spirit ride, the red background. Eleanor liked that the red blanket would always remind her of the red rocks of the canyon.

Then she went on to explore the Spirit in other places. She made it all the way to the Pacific Ocean. She stopped at an isolated stretch of beach. The wind was pushing her to the water, where a pony pranced in tumult with the waves. She felt his body throb. She ran alongside, legs beating up and down in unison, feeling connected with the very first people. How wildly excited they must have been to discover such a vast expanse. They would dance, then sit around the campfire where they told the very first stories. The thought of the campfire crackled and conjured ancient memories of "The First Blanket," an ancient creation story. All came into being out of necessity. Ancestors whispered the reasons for her name. Eleanor was a lonely old Aunt who said she was not lonely. The wind lifted her arms. Gave her freedom. From then on she spoke to herself from the inside, carrying the Wind and Pony Spirits always.

The Rambler broke down in California. She drank a PBR in salute of the old car, a gesture of farewell, and dribbled a splash of beer on the hood in preparation for the scrapyard. Eleanor smiled at the Rambler's journey from a christening of champagne in early Charles days to a burial of beer. She got on a Greyhound back to the Midwest before her money ran out. The whole bus ride home she was comforted and entertained by her own deepened reflection in the glass that looked both in and out. She held the Navajo blanket close around her shoulders. She fingered the red diamond rock pattern. The white pony lifted off the blanket and ran alongside the Greyhound. The throb of the canter thundered over the waves. Her heart beat in incantation like a drum.

Starkweather Creek

my saw that a man with long hair, a beard, and a crazy hat moved into a converted barbershop down the block. The red-and-white-striped barber sign was still in the window. He introduced himself to her as George, and when they took their first walk together the bright yellow lettering on his black tee shirt said "magick." Watch out, she thought, a charmer. They went to a park by the big lake. They were sitting on top of a picnic table looking at the photos in George's wallet: his mom, his sister, his daughter. He was divorced. The daughter had lived in New Mexico with her mother. A space heater in the daughter's bedroom had killed her. The ex had gotten out through a bathroom window. His voice split open: "Jenny. Always with me." Amy liked that his hand caressed the girl's face.

A sudden gust of wind picked up his hat and flung it out into open water. Ducks began swimming over to investigate. George lowered himself into the water by the pier and dog-paddled out to his hat. He clutched the brim in his teeth like a retriever, paddled lopsidedly back, plopped it onto the pier. With great effort he pulled himself up onto land, breathing heavily. "I don't swim well," he told her.

The retrieval had smitten Amy. Later she learned he had won the hat in a poker game. He had worn the crushed felt fedora his senior year of college and all through his painful marriage in New Mexico, and then the divorce. The hat sat, an embattled trophy on top of his lush hair. He seldom removed it.

Amy and George eventually married. There was a photo of their daughter Gwen's baptism, George proudly holding Gwen who was wearing the traditional gown his mother had sent. Of all the many family photos taken over the years, it was one of few she found of him without his hat.

*   *   *

In the autumn of their life together Amy would realize George was really sick when he no longer cared about his hat. At his funeral she placed it on his chest, between his hands. Then they closed the casket. Winter of her life, a frozen stark stupor.

Years passed, and Amy was helping Gwen plan her wedding. While Gwen and her fiancé Alex stood in line to claim a midsummer spot at Olbrich Garden, Amy walked the garden paths, remembering. She had purchased two bricks for the pathway leading to the rose garden. One said "George Amy/Breese Inn." Breese because their home was right next to Breese Stephens Field and they listened to many exciting sports events and rock concerts through the walls of their dwelling. The other brick said "Gwen Wren/ Brew Shoe." Wren was her special nickname for Gwen, a bird in chattering flight. She thought of the Beatles song "Blackbird," how Gwen too, with her dark African skin, struggled to be free. "Brew Shoe" was the endearing name for their rescue dog. Brew was into leather, and by habit they took their shoes off when entering the house and put them on top of the refrigerator.

Amy noticed the old window washer from State Street seated on a bench between two hippies, the Stones booming from their radio. Campus gentrification must have pushed him this far east. They had chosen a public place for the ceremony, and, as the ceremony approached she would welcome this venerable old man and his ragtag friends. At the place of entrance and departure she noticed his intent eyes enlivened by the reflection pool.

Gwen began her preparations, placing small white banners on each side of the pathway next to their bricks. Amy walked over to the young couple, felt the imprint of their life on the soles of her feet. George had come back to her before, in the form of wild birds clawing their way home. He was here now in a calmer way. She knew he would be with them when she walked their daughter down the pathway. He would be with them when Gwen and Alex walked back after the ceremony. He had guided their daughter into adulthood. He had consoled his wife after he left. Amy understood that he would walk along the pathway, out through the back door, and then keep going.

After the reception and the dancing and a few glasses of wine, Amy felt a relaxed pull downward. Everyone agreed it had been a great party. Gwen and Alex were on their way. The flagged bricks had been a hit. The guests had all felt George's presence. Amy and her friends, Eleanor and Maddy, crossed the bridge over Starkweather Creek to find their cars. Amy drove back to her apartment down the street.

She poured herself one shot of brandy, neat, and raised her glass in the direction she thought George might go: north, further out each time, flying above the ravages of stark weather. She put on her granny nightgown and flopped into her soft bed. It was easier than some nights to drift off to sleep, the gauze light against her skin, her brain circuitry orchestrating release, a quiver of wings.

She awoke the next morning from a deep sleep and made coffee to charge her day. Smells percolated the air. She noticed that last night she had forgotten to screw the top back on the brandy bottle. Fruit flies had hitchhiked from the farmer's market and set up domestic relationships in her apartment. The open bottle had invited whole families to dive-bomb into the brandy, perishing, sodden. She slowly poured the brandy down the sink drain. One fruit fly had defied the abyss, her body immobile on the kitchen counter, wings extended in debauched ecstasy. She gently touched an index finger to the fruit fly and placed her on a white napkin. There, through the coming brilliant and harsh months, Amy would appreciate her dark body, open wings, her sheer joy.

Learn to Fly

They had all been mainstays in their neighborhood for many years, had gardened together and raked together and shoveled together. Each early fall the neighbors organized a block party, obtained a city license to get the street closed off to traffic, went all out with food and music and children's games. Faces of many hues mingled, free from the chains of judgment. There was always a piñata. The adults looked forward to catching the sweets almost as much as the kids.

Eleanor volunteered to try and find some musicians for the block party. She had been impressed with the band at her friend Amy's daughter's wedding reception. The band had inspired her to get out there on the dance floor. She and Amy and their new friend Maddy took an aqua Zumba class together three times a week at the Y and began to feel more confident in their ability to move with the music. The three friends surprised the twenty-somethings at the wedding with their ability to move to the sound of the band, grizzled codgers stroking beats out of familiar and also more recent tunes. That band, Electric Wail, was known for playing covers of famous old songs, songs that still rang through everyone's heads up at the Harmony Bar, where the musicians ensconced themselves on Sunday afternoons.

The short walk up to the Harmony that Sunday exhilarated her. She almost hated to go inside a dark bar on such a glorious day. But Eleanor was determined to ask the band if they might volunteer a Saturday afternoon at the local block party. She sat at a table in the back room and ordered herself a beer. The band was just beginning to set up on stage. She thought she would have more clout with them if she listened to the music first. The band was sure to take a break. She would plead her case at that time and then make her escape.

It was easy to sit in the front row and listen to the familiar songs reverberating through her head. The lead singer was quite good and the guitars really did wail. The mixed crowd of young and old around her was better than any advertisement or business card. She sipped her beer and began to relax. Each old cover song brought up a memory of the men who had been in her life. "Hello, Goodbye" conjured up her first husband, dead way too early. She was happy to sit for a fleeting moment and think about him. The songs quickly turned into each other. As with other meditative times, her head began again to recite her litany of disappointing men. Dark thoughts led her to Charles when she heard "If Dogs Run Free." He was too weak to stand up to the strong woman she was becoming. He left her, even left their sweet dog. That thought led to her dear dog Frankie, who, like all the dogs in her life, helped her through the rough parts.

She heard a few Beatles songs from the White Album that brought her joy and pleasure. The lads knew how to tell a good story. Then "Your Bird Can Sing" took her to an adventurous, desolate stop with Travis in Arizona. A real travesty of a relationship. He couldn't stand to lose at cards or arguments and left her in the lurch. She remembered how she had headed for car breakdown and self-discovery in California. She had gone through pain to feel free.

Electric Wail announced that there would be a ten-minute intermission. Eleanor gave them time to rest, then approached the lead singer.

"I've heard you at the Harmony before. I was at the wedding reception you played a few weekends ago. You really got us old gals out there on the dance floor."

His furrowed face looked surprised. Then he smiled. "Oh. That was a fun time. The people were so down home." His voice was deep and enticing.

It gave her the liberty to ask: "My neighbors and I were wondering if you guys would ever consider playing at our Saturday afternoon block party in a few weeks? We're just down the street from here. Of course we're working class, so it would have to be a volunteer gift . . . Maybe we could pass a hat for beer money."

Again his face registered surprise, as if she were some foreign agent. "I'll have to huddle with my bandmates. Then I promise to give you an answer. Can I have your name and phone number or e-mail address?"

Her hand was shaking as she dug in her purse for a pen and a piece of paper. She could tell it would take a couple of days for four diverse and opinionated musicians to arrive at a consensus.

"Thank you for your consideration. We so enjoy your songs." Electric Wail had indeed leap-frogged others' words into their own world. Eleanor smiled an encouraging smile and handed him her information. She left the band alone for the rest of their break. Eleanor didn't want to be a clinging groupie. She finished her last inch of beer. The lights were coming back on. It was time to return home in that glorious sun. She got up from her front row chair and headed for the door. The band began to play "Blackbird," her favorite Beatles song of all time, pure poetry.

She sat down in the back row and hung onto every word and sound. Her thoughts flew inward.

The broken wings strengthen and mend and the bird learns to fly again. Her life was waiting for the moment of healing to arrive. The dark black night was the time for her mind's healing flight. She saw herself merge with the night and find bird, wing, song, appear again in a distant tree filled with circles of her strong age. The song emerged from the wailing guitars and she was left with the sense of black brilliance. Black students had been set free from discrimination. A cure had occurred in the merger between the felt and the known world. She knew that life was after all not the disappointments Charles, Travis, and other men had imposed. Life, if she waited and listened, could actually be quite exceedingly good. Ordering another beer, Eleanor stayed for the rest of the concert.

In the strokes of red sky on her walk home she felt the empowerment of mended wings. And sure enough, in a few days the singer from Electric Wail, who introduced himself as Tom, called to say the band had agreed to do the block party gig.

"We can always use beer money." His voice was deep and clear.

On the day of the party Eleanor prepared her famous bread, Vienna sliced part way through and stuffed with butter, garlic, Swiss cheese, and mushrooms. She brought it over warm from the oven and people dove into all the good food. Electric Wail showed up and people of all shapes and colors were in heaven. The kind guy with the challenged child raised and lowered the piñata according to each person's ability. The daughter's delighted smile told her how he set his daughter free from discrimination about her disability.

At the end of the evening, Eleanor sat on her front stoop chatting with the venerable old neighbor she sometimes gardened with. The woman paused to pick pieces of saltwater taffy out of her store-bought teeth. A good piece of candy could take you places. Eleanor was in flight and felt she had to tell her old neighbor. They had mended their friendship after sputtering over opposing political yard signs.

"The saltwater taffy suggests to me that you are swimming along the waters of a Long Island beach. Free from obstacles."

The women laughed. Eleanor drank her last sip of beer. Electric Wail thanked the crowd for passing the hat. They closed out their gig with "Blackbird." Eleanor thought of the song's deeper meaning: how the black birds were the discriminated students in Little Rock fighting against segregation, waiting for their freedom to arrive. Birds, neighbors, assumed disabilities flew free in this moment.

Boxcar Blues

Louise came back to her apartment after their trip to Olbrich Gardens consumed with the expectations of harvest. She remembered the pleasure of sitting on their usual bench, this time witnessing the wedding ceremony of a lovely young couple. Her rapscallion troupe was on their best behavior, showed respect for the new adventures ahead. On their way onward the couple stood at the reflection pool. She watched Mr. Bojangles' eyes follow their path. Her Rip had his hair slicked back in the most endearing way. Louise honored the moment, a harvest of memory, a promise of garden.

The hearty hibiscus she had planted at the back entrance to her apartment building last Spring opened yellow cups to accept the sunshine. That plant was her welcome home. She liked that none of the other dwellers thought to pluck those glorious yellow tropical blossoms for only themselves. How generous flowers could be for this Wisconsin community! Butterflies and bees helped them thrive.

It was getting late enough in the day for her to know her own bounty. With her ragtag clothes she was already dressed for the occasion. On her walk home Rip had fingered that make-shift slide of her shirt. She felt his touch all the way inside. But then he was saying he did not want to help her with the harvest. The community garden plot she rented down by the railroad tracks beckoned. Rip wanted nothing to do with community. A train whistle was his only calling. He stood in front of her with the window washer Mr. Bojangles. His words still rang in her ears.

"Your new attempts at growing stuff reminds me too much of my commune days. My parents quickly turned naked frivolity into sweaty labor. This was called survival."

He paused on their walk back from Olbrich to touch her face.

"The naked part I love. You bring me to my most frivolous self. But I will never be a sweaty laborer."

Then he had parted from her. Mr. Bojangles, limping from arthritis in his knees, followed him. Louise faced her facts. People survived as best they could. As did that old dog Wally who had always followed along. As did her daughter wearing her new toddler shoes until her legs didn't work anymore. She was beginning to need the stability of a return to hibiscus in one place. So she decided to carry her vagabonds with her even when they were away. Louise hoisted her hoe, left her apartment, walked the three blocks down to the railroad tracks, remembering how Mr. Bojangles had always held his window washing squeegee like a bayonet. She got to work in her community garden plot, putting all her energy into the hoeing. Her own sweat felt like the yearn of sexual desire coming up through the roots of the plants.

The darkening sky promised another bright day tomorrow. Red lines veined the air. The water spigot was ready to do its work. Louise crunched down on a sweet red pepper, tasted membranes and flesh and seed in her mouth. She wiped away the residue and stood back to admire her accomplishment. Hearing a train sound warning, Louise thought of one of the few western songs she really loved: "I'm So Lonesome I Could Cry." She could see worms working the earth, luxuriating in the dampness. She gave the red pepper its final crunch.

Rip and Mr. Bojangles were approaching, headed for the tracks. They snuck under the railroad gate. The train screeched to a halt in front of them, waiting for a signal. City folk were used to waiting for the train switch. She remembered the young hippie who years ago had hopped off the boxcar on Johnson Street and asked her: "Which way is State Street?" Street people went back a long way, just as innocent back then. She saw Rip tenderly lift a foot and begin to place Mr. Bojangles on the rung of the ladder. She went over to help push him up. He was able to do some of the work. Even though his fingers were curved from arthritis, his arms were still strong from all his days of window washing. Rip got his knees to work up the rung and he let out a triumphant grunt. Both of her loved men were seated on some straw in the open box car. She got down off the ladder to the sound of click and clack. Gears shifted. She stood back as the yellow railroad cars gathered speed. Louise counted the names and loves as the train slowly lurched forward: "Eddie. Jackie. Johnny Cash. Wear it black." The four-letter words of gang wars. All the ruffians looking for comfort: "Zone me."

Louise leaned against her hoe, cheek resting on the top of the handle. She knew Rip wanted to guide their dear Mr. Bojangles south before winter. He would be back sometime. Rip had a history of return. Over the next months she thought of her two men every time she heard a train whistle. She was a zone; he would need to get back to her. There would come a time when she again heard Rip's gentle insistent knock on her door. He would kiss her closed eyes, touch her face, go down there, take her to the places he had been.

Take Heed

Maddy awoke with the armful of words she had gathered from yesterday's wedding wrapped across her chest. She remembered "Uptown Funk" best. The words handed her honesty: "Don't believe me, just watch." She wanted to strum out into the world noticing what people did, not what they said. She needed to find a new audience to try out her lyrics. People were important even if she only saw them a time or two.

Her Sunday ritual was reading the newspaper and being lazy. Today would be different. The wedding of Amy's charming daughter Gwen to that handsome young man had energized her. Now that her old love Stuart was gone, she had to find other ways to meet people. She looked in the newspaper to find the Sunday Open Houses. In the special section on lake property she found a house within walking distance.

The air was crisp with promised gifts. The house sat at the top of a hill with windows peering out over the lake. It had a strip of public land in front of it, so property taxes would be a little less, although the whole quest was in honesty not possible on her limited senior citizen income. She would pretend to be a serious buyer just to dream about the possibilities. Her face crinkled with curiosity. She wondered if the real estate agent would see through her ploy.

The front porch had a handrail, perfect for her arthritic knees, and the foyer opened up to the welcoming living area. Dressed in the suit of success, the smiling woman guided her forward. Vanilla candles and fresh baked cookies provided a homey smell that lured her in. Windows opened her eyes; the view was everything. The lake outside began to tell the secrets of the people who came before. A newly restored Native American totem, bear merging with bird enfolding man, invited her to look deeply into the waters. Just watch. Sail away. She began to find her songs in this place.

Maddy now said her first words of the day. She wanted to sing them, but didn't want to confuse the generously smiling realtor or the other people looking in awe at the house. "Thank you for showing me this fantastic place. You'll have no trouble selling it." She inserted a lilt into her voice. Maybe the agent shared some of her Irish heritage. She felt that she had jump-started her troubadour spirit for the day.

She used that well-placed handrail on the way down, swinging her purse from side to side for balance on her walk to the bus stop. Stuart had always admonished her for her "luggage of a purse," but now he had packed his own bag and was gone. She used the purse as a Native American would a large stitched fold of birch bark for carrying messages. Today it carried a CD, a fundraiser for the Fiftieth Anniversary of Amnesty International. Last night she had listened to all four discs, all contemporary covers of old Bob Dylan songs. She had embedded his words in her head as a young woman. Three of the discs were perfect. But that first disc was flawed. Voices wavered on "Not Dark Yet," then skipped, then began repeating from "Boots of Spanish Leather" to the end. The Airborne Toxic Event's heartfelt rendition about loving someone enough to let them go was ruined. The ghost boots went on trudging the earth alone. She had begun to cry when she heard the disconnect.

She was organized enough to have kept her sales receipt. Today was the last day to make an exchange or return. Since the CD was a fundraiser, she guessed that no clerk would offer a replacement. She swung the purse carrying her treasure onto the bus, heard her coins chime against each other in the receptacle. The bus driver gave her a big smile. They knew each other from years of rides. Maddy liked the fact that the driver was Muslim, still wore her hijab, and pushed the boundaries of her conservative faith by choosing to drive a bus for her occupation. Many's the time she represented her faith by helping Maddy and other older folk on and off the bus. The bus was half empty. She chose a seat near the front and began to sing under her breath, then louder: "Your thoughts are not with me. . ." She knew enough about Bob Dylan to beware of stormy weather. Sometimes you have to let your love sail away. The action of genuine love. "Send me boots, Dylan asked for boots of Spanish leather as a gift of remembrance." His words quelled her bitterness toward Stuart. The bus driver gave her a big grin when she helped her down the stairs: "Thanks for the lyrics."

The bus stop was only a few steps from the entrance to Best Buy. She stood in the customer service line. Finally an extremely young and nervous clerk asked if he could help.

"There is a defect on disc one. Perhaps it sat too long in a shipping crate. Or perhaps a production worker, reveling in the Bob Dylan spirit, spilled some burgundy wine on the edges."

He looked at her. She could see his face doubt the accuracy of the inept older woman standing in front of him. He walked over to one of the store CD machines and began playing the disc. The music played beautifully through "Not Dark Yet." She began to think the problem was in her CD player at home. It was about twenty years old. She found room in the slant of light of Silversun Pickup's interpretation. She watched the young clerk's face change from doubt to admiration. She wasn't about to tell him that she had never heard of Silversun Pickups or The Airborne Toxic Events before. She was in it for the words. A few people gathered to listen and it made the troubadour in her glad. The CD was a fundraiser for Amnesty International.

But "Boots of Spanish Leather" did skip and repeat. She saw the clerk shift his corporate capitalist stance. He called a manager. The CD was flawed and she got her exchange.

On the bus ride home she tried to take heed of Dylan's words. Stuart sailed away forever across coastal Spain. She would have to gift herself her own boots.

The exchanged CD turned out to be perfect. She enjoyed many hours of pleasure. Saved up her coins every day to buy a pair of leather boots for winter.

Start Me Up

Greyhound had halted service to many small towns, but they still swung into Eau Claire before traveling on to Minneapolis. Louise found it harder than ever to leave her flowers and vegetables in Madison, but now that it was late March and time to plan her garden in her mind, she had agreed to go. Rip always had that itch to travel.

They saved their money and bought two round-trip tickets to Eau Claire to get as far as they could into northern Wisconsin before the bus swung west toward the Twin Cities. The two vagabonds settled back in their bus seats to study a map. Louise noticed the sweet curve of Rip's palm as he held the map up for her to see the possibilities. They whispered and decided that when the bus made an announced pit stop in Hixton they would get off. Eau Claire was a bit too big for their tastes. On the three-hour trip Louise shivered when she saw a dead deer by the side of the road, its legs stiffened in the frozen ground as if in animal prayer. Every time Louise looked sideways she saw another member of the herd stiffened in the Wisconsin cold. If she had believed in God she would have thought He was calling the deer home. As it was, she hadn't been in a church in years. Mick Jagger preached the only religion she knew. Through the bus window she heard the March wind, a high priest blowing music. Where were the deer going? Rip put his arm around her and that helped.

The bus pulled into the small hamlet of Hixton for a McDonald's break. The fast food place sat next to the only gas station in the unincorporated town. Louise and Rip grabbed their small bags and never looked back. Other than the restaurant and a run-down bar the town didn't seem to have much. A person looked at them and frowned as they walked down the street crunching snow.

Louise was a bar person and she was glad to walk into the Buzz Inn. Rip followed cautiously. He'd been kicked out of bars before. It was just about noon, so okay to have their first beer of the day. The jukebox was twanging mournful country tunes and the travelers needed to cheer themselves up. When Louise closed her eyes she saw again the dead deer.

The bar was occupied by a few bearded woodsmen who sat crouched over their drinks, seeming to relish the loneliness of their backwoods life. The face of the middle-aged woman behind the bar brightened when she saw the two strangers walk in. It was by no stretch of the imagination a fancy craft beer kind of place, but the new arrivals smiled when they saw that Leinenkugel's was on tap. Chippewa Falls! How much more local can you get?

Louise and Rip raised their glasses to the bartender and so the banter began. It turned out that Meghan the bartender was a local who just never felt the need to get out of Hixton. The Buzz gave her steady work, even in the winter. A few of the bearded men managed to hop on their Harleys and make it to the bar most days. Louise sensed their set, simple lives. It was what she had been aiming for in Madison with her vegetable garden and ensemble of wayward street people. Rip was more of an adventurer, inclined to hop a train to anywhere.

Meghan told them about a church on the outskirts of town. The local young priest went against his bishop's rule and let people scrub and crash. He never locked the doors. He was in charge of the church in another parish too, so wasn't in Hixton often. Meghan confided that nobody in the area locked their door except the bar, the gas station, and the McDonald's. Louise thought maybe the unlocked doors meant that people trusted each other here. That was not the case in Madison; she had made sure her precious radio and CD player were locked up tight before she left.

The pews were hard wood, so they spread their rolled-up bedding on the floor. It was okay because it brought Louise back to her street-living days, where she had acquired her life skills: self-preservation and loyalty to friends. She had first met sweet Rip on the streets just before she got her first low-income place. People living day to day made her shift the "they" to "us." Louise had her history in mind as she and Rip began their week of rituals: the walks, their breaths turned to frost in the morning sunlight and again turning to condensation under the glow of the solitary streetlight. Their religious rituals were fast food, the Buzz, and the church.

One day a youngish woman walked into the bar and sat next to one of the gruff, bearded woodsmen. Within the hour her tears were flowing as fast as her beer. Patsy Cline on the jukebox had the young woman drowning in sorrow. Louise always thought Patsy Cline too talented to be that sorrowful. But then again she was singing for all country women. Louise started wanting to get back to her rock and roll in Madison. The small line of bearded men on barstools was soon circling the crying woman, trying to console her. Except for the man she had chosen to sit next to. All anyone could see was the back of his red-and-black checkered wool shirt. Louise and Meghan were the only other women in the place. Louise felt like they had to stick together. Meghan leaned over the young woman in motherly attention. She tapped her hand lightly: "Glad to meet you." Louise thought she looked too young to be in the bar, but there were no cops around. The weeping girl blurted out her name: her broken voice said "Thelma." Louise felt a special connection because of the movie "Thelma and Louise." All women wanted was to establish their boundaries for how men could behave. Hopefully they didn't have to cause harm to get their message across. Louise remembered paying special attention to the Louise in the movie saying "when a woman's crying like that, she ain't having any fun." She decided to offer Thelma a hand:

"Hey Thelma, want to go to the ladies' room with me? We can splash some cold water on our faces."

Thelma nodded in child-like agreement. Once in the ladies' room she emitted a deeper sob.

"That dude is my boyfriend. Or at least I thought he was."

Louise gave her a hug and Thelma's story came pouring out of her like spilt beer. It seems that last night at dusk deer had wandered into their backyard. Thelma talked about how they were so close she saw their eyelashes flash in the beam of lights from their living room window. Her man had said "I need supper" and shot a doe, dropping her in her tracks. Thelma ran to see if the doe was really dead. There was no quiver of a heartbeat in the still warm body. She felt further down and knew instinctively that the bulge meant a fawn would now never be born. Her stranger of a man hung the deer and her precious cargo with pride on the eaves of the garage. The knife came later.

Thelma's sobs increased to a yearning wail. She wanted life in her own body. Her boyfriend was older, had a son, and had said an emphatic "no way." In a pained, halting voice, she described their fall motorcycle trip to Eau Claire. Her belly felt every thump in the road. Louise watched her cradle her belly in stillborn grief. A piece of Thelma was gone for good in the scalpel of the big city. They had cut the whole embryo out. She would never get it back. Louise knew deep down that Thelma's was no survival-of-the-fittest saga. People up here were enclosed and selfish. If knives were the reality of backwoods living she would leave it behind. Entrenched men in hick towns thought it "manly" to scorn their women. She couldn't wait to get back to Madison. There her street people set their own boundaries, but they knew enough to stick together. She thought lovingly of her man waiting patiently at the bar. Rip was all about return. She used a paper towel to wipe away Thelma's tears.

"Do you want to hop a bus back to Madison with me and Rip? We've got a bit of money left."

"I'll see. I want to give my man a second chance." Thelma seemed tuned in to Patsy Cline's "Crazy."

Louise thought "She'll stay, just like Meghan." When they got back to their barstools she watched Thelma nudge her boyfriend. He swung his stool around. They struggled into their heavy coats and left the Buzz together. The next day Meghan was busy at the Buzz, cleaning up yesterday's mess. She had not seen Thelma, but promised to look out for her. There was also no sign of Thelma at the McDonald's. She must have accepted her backwoods fate. Rock and roll music began an insistent drumming inside Louise, stretching her mind. Mick Jagger's "Start Me Up" could teach a grown man how to cry proper tears. As had been announced when they bought their round-trip tickets, a bus pulled into Hixton. Louise and Rip flagged down the Greyhound and started for home.

Honeybees

There was nothing like a generous squeeze of honey from Amy's bear bottle to liven up her breakfast yogurt. She had learned to buy local honey. Amy had allergies and local bees went foraging for the very clover and flowers that made her sneeze, and thus their honey helped strengthen her immune system. She felt a sneeze attack surfacing, helped herself to the one squeeze left.

After her itchy nose and eyes subsided she walked over to her neighbor's house. Jerry kept bees and they made fantastic honey. He called his business Princess Honey. His wife was the Queen and their little girl his Princess. Opening the front door with less fanfare than usual, Jerry slowly shook his head back and forth, a frown on his face. When Amy saw his price list she raised her eyes in wonder. The price for one small bottle had more than doubled.

"Bee populations are way down. Flowers are offering nectar, but there are fewer takers. Workers are flying off to die alone. Pesticides. Climate change."

Amy heard the sad tone in Jerry's voice. His beekeeping was as much a hobby as a business, but think of the people who tended beehives for their livelihood. She wanted to know more about the decline. For the moment she merely dug out extra money. Natural allergy immunity was worth the price. She vowed to replenish the honey by polishing up her writing. Make her words more publishable.

The next morning she was grateful for her new bear bottle. Her eyes had crusted up overnight. The honey brought relief. She squeezed some of the precious golden liquid in her tea, too. This bottle was not going to last long.

Amy used her cleared head to write a new story. Bees were the star characters. They had devolved from prolific to lethargic. For research she returned to Silent Spring to try to find out why. She again walked with Rachel Carson through orchards, pondering the loss of bird sounds, observing, merging poetry and science. As a young college student Rachel collected poetry rejection slips like silenced bird trills held as warnings inside her shoebox. In graduate school she gathered data on pesticides invading every link in the food chain. She was a woman ahead of her time. Amy could see the results today. Flowers held their flutes of nectar up for disappearing pollinators. Clover and hay waited all spring to germinate.

Amy pondered the population decline. Surely pesticides were still a culprit. Chemicals weakened immune systems. If it was happening to the bees it would eventually happen to humans. She read that Rachel Carson gave up her academic career to work for the US Fish and Wildlife Service. The poet/scientist foresaw our current plight. Amy looked up honeybee decline. She learned that in 2017 Fish and Wildlife added the rusty patched bumblebee to the endangered species list.

She brought her newly acquired information to Jerry, her beekeeper neighbor.

"Yep. It's all true. Had a bad winter, too. Lost 30%. That winter vortex came swooping through town. "

erry's confirmation reminded her that Rachel Carson had warned that climate change was another culprit. She remembered the recent extreme seasons here in the Midwest: stark cold, dry springs, blasts of heat, leaves losing the energy to change colors. On the east and west coasts, squalls eating the land brought flood and mud. The character of winds changed with the seasons, blowing hot and dry on both coasts. Then humans flicked cigarettes and crackling fires began. Californians suffered. The burning in Tennessee meant Dolly Parton felt compelled to come to the rescue.

Amy decided to help the bees in her own humble way. She planted flowers, cultivated a patch of clover, set out sugar water. When some of her neighbors saw her new yard projects they began their own rituals of survival.

She endured many more seasons of weather extremes. The honey bear squeeze bottle was low, perpetually low. She would have to dig deep to buy another supply. Amy found her most recent story. She created a bee busy buzzing inside a can of soda. Her old self would have put a lid on it until the danger of a sting was over. Her new self waited patiently until the bee flew away free. It seemed to talk to her in its joyful buzz flight.

"You could fill your little cup with me."

The bee character energized her story. Amy came to understand that she was writing the story for Rachel Carson. She would free her heroine from a shoebox of rejection slips by celebrating her merger of poetry and science. The bee dialogue continued when its fuzz of a yellow pulsating body flew down into her patch of purple clover (an Honor!). Amy plucked one stem and sucked on the sweetness, the August sun beating down on the bee's flight path. It flew busily among the purple offerings. She told the bee that the Queen would be pleased with her worker.

As she walked through her neighborhood to buy another in a long line of squeeze bears, a squadron of honey strong enough for any farmers market, she felt proud to be doing her small part for the chain of being. Her writing was polished by the buzz of bees. She thought about the lid finally lifted off the shoebox.

Jerry's big grin told her he was back to his magnanimous self. He said production was a little bit better. Perhaps the pollinators were not on a downward spiral. He handed her the precious supply of liquid gold. But then on her way back home she passed by plats of neon-green well-manicured lawns. Not a yellow wild-maned dandelion in sight. She faced another season without her dandelion wine. She saw bright bursts still glorious by the side of the road clustered around a warning sign: TREATED. KEEP OFF THE GRASS! Amy could just about hear the fade of the bee buzz upon the sprayed pristine landscape.

Deluge

The Yahara River had overflown its banks. Lake Monona was pouring into the rich peoples' basements. Lake Mendota stopped traffic along Tenney Park. The arched bridge between the lake and the creek gave way to the force of water. Louise made it as far as Olbrich Gardens and found the white birch bark rotting on the trunks, too wet to write a message on in the Native American tradition she liked to follow. The street people didn't know where to hang out. Tree roots were weakened by weeks of rain. She watched a guy maneuver his bike around fallen limbs, water surging up around his tires.

Her arms ached to hoe in her garden down by the railroad tracks, but that was a ruination of water. She shivered as she knelt to pull her big boot box from under her bed. Shoeboxes always reminded her of former life, her dear sweet child going up and down, pumping the swing in her toddler shoes. Her daughter had gone to the grave years ago; that life stored upon the dusty back shelf of her maternal mind. Louise pulled on her hip-deep heavy rubber boots to wade downhill and further inspect her garden. She felt every sloosh, fingered upturned lettuce, leaves and roots dangling like so many greenish worms. She held lifeless dragon beans. Tomatoes had dropped to the ground to be buried alive in mud. She could only imagine the vegetables' gasps for air. Even her hearty zucchini gave up ghosts. The river was too deep. The lakes were full of blue/green algae. Her fisherman and lover Rip suffered in silence. Where was the sustenance?

The social worker assigned to her apartment building helped with the application for food stamps. Louise was not used to needing assistance in the summer. She prided herself on growing her own food. But Joyce convinced her that, in this extreme weather, she should accept help. Joyce even helped Rip, who wasn't really her responsibility because he refused to live under a roof. He had tried living in Louise's low-income building, then scoffed: "My mind tells me what kind of roof I live under."

There was only one checkout line at the grocery store that accepted food stamps. Louise and Rip had been granted the measly amount of fifteen dollars a month each. That might cover a little protein, vegetables, and dairy. But the disastrous rains had ruined many crops and prices were high. Louise wondered if she would ever be able to return to the productivity of her garden. She stood in the slowly moving line and worried about the problems: Storms. Heat. Fires. Swells of wind and water. Then in winter would come a vortex of frigid air.

The street people she knew from years past had no answers for the extreme weather. They just lived their lives from minute to minute, a comradery Rip seemed to feel with every hobo. He liked to share cans of beans down by the railroad tracks. The worst was when, on a whim, he hopped a train for a free ride. Louise worried he would take off again soon. She tried to draw him into her orbit.

They left the grocery store together and Louise offered an observation: "Trains have roofs and walls too. We're all boxed in, if we let ourselves be."

Rip's break-free grin surged them forward. He nudged her shoulder with his small grocery bag and began heading toward her apartment, a good sign.

Once there, safely on the third floor away from prying eyes, Louise pulled off her hip wader boots and set them on the register to dry. Rip pulled off his waterproof poncho, the one Louise really liked because it made him look like a mysterious bandit. They delved into the groceries, made a feast of cheese and string beans.

Louise's arms ached for Rip as much as for her garden. Sitting back on the couch, the two watched the local news. Rip didn't pay much attention to the news unless he was with her. She always wanted to hear the weather report. Today's weatherman looked like a regular street person. He reported that the rain was supposed to continue off-and-on all month. She liked that television was getting away from plastic faces. She was more likely to believe the words of a non-puppet person. Louise realized they would have to ration their grocery supplies, decided right then and there not to give Rip her opinion. The lack of provisions would make him hop the next train out of here.

He put his arm around her shoulder. Louise snuggled back into the thrill of his touch. Funny how it was different each time and she never knew how it was going to be. They were both going into memories of their separate teenage lives: experimental touching in the back of some dilapidated Chevy, or the power control in the back of a Studebaker Hawk. After a long time Louise knew it was only going to go this far. She was fine with it, felt that same young-woman tingle of long ago. She was glad Rip was nothing like that early dictator boyfriend, the one who accepted no responsibility for their baby. Her child's shoes swung back into vision. Louise never had any question about keeping her daughter. They had been a team from the beginning. Sometimes she tried to explain her past to Rip, but mostly she kept it to herself. He never really heard what she was saying. Street people required tough skins and there were times when her skin felt elastic clarity, like she could see everything that was happening within.

She heard the rain relent. Rip must have heard it too: He stood up and stretched, kissed her on the cheek, headed for his poncho. "Got to clear my head, find the right roof." She could still feel that tingle on her cheek. The damp kiss traveled up to that dusty shelf inside her head.

Some things were best remembered in that solitary action she called deluge-of-mind. She fingered her rubber boots. Dry. She genuflected at the foot of her bed, pulled out her boot box. When she lifted the lid to replace her waders, toddler shoes swung into her vision. It was time again for revival. Her daughter emerged from the confines of her mind. Louise carefully set the boots upright, outside the box, ready to jump into for the upcoming deluge.

Owl

Eleanor wondered why Arthur, an engineer by profession, was attracted to her. In the beginning she found him interesting, a counterpoint to the frivolous actress in her. She had become numb then strangely flippant after the death of her husband Ray twelve years ago. Her daughter Alice had frozen up for a while, then freed herself in college. Eleanor thought maybe a second marriage was the defrost cycle of her life, but second husband Charles had been a disaster, a ruination from which she learned she had to be with a man who matched her strength. She pretended that flirtatious Arthur cared about her and was surprised when he responded with sunflowers and a stuffed animal, an owl which she perched on her sofa pillow for cuddling when he was here drawing his structures and when he was away building them.

One day she came home from lunch at a Chinese restaurant. She was a sucker for believing the message in her fortune cookie. She wanted to know what "You will have a happy life" might mean. She hoped it meant "happy" for herself and for Alice. Arthur was more of a realist. He was a wiry guy who wound his way around questions. He possessed the practicality of a rotary router.

"Don't you know after all these years of living you don't need a fortune teller? You can make your own life."

His voice had the edge of a scoff in it that annoyed Eleanor. Precision was his imperative. For Eleanor, a paper prediction of "Happy life" became a burst of sunflowers spinning petal compasses. He thought sunflowers were sunflowers. The glass-eyed stuffed owl with glints of sun stared from its perch on her couch. Arthur's voice broke in upon her yellow compass.

"Don't you see that not everything is a symbol? Be happy with the owl as it is, a stuffed childish toy."

He was deriding her now. Well, he was wired for precision, a robotic tinkerer, while she was all open flow. She was up late. He lay turned away from her in a huff. Eleanor decided that she shouldn't live with him anymore. It was a physical warning: she felt frozen, needed large gulps of air, gasping to be free of him. He could retreat into his workaholic self. She just didn't care anymore.

Arthur took some time to tell her he was married, as if that could justify all the times the owl waited on the couch. Had she known, she never would have been with him. She was relieved when he moved back in with his wife. Eleanor now understood she had been his mid-life crisis prize. Instead of a red convertible, she had been frivolous enough to distract him from the fact that his life was more than half over.

She enjoyed another Chinese lunch and read her fortune cookie. It said "You will go on a journey and come to a great wall. You will climb over this wall." Was this the Great Wall of China? She knew American-Chinese restaurants weren't authentic Chinese. Plus she knew she was no longer agile enough to climb over a wall.

She sat in her backyard to contemplate what the message might mean. Soon, an owl appeared overhead and landed on the upper branch of a pine tree. The owl began to appear to her often in the early evening. She could see the energy of his body beat, a beacon from within.

She started reading and listening to everything she could about owls. Mary Oliver's owl of knowledge. A lecture at the Aldo Leopold Nature Center. Her own personal owl flew above, wings reaching new heights. The backyard sky was getting dark but she could see the beam of his yellow owl eyes. His flight lifted her over the wall. The owl scaled a tree to the very top, prey on his radar, eyes and head rotating. A helpless harem of rabbits huddled near a tree stump, twitching, frozen. The rabbits made a clumsy scurry toward the blocked journey. When the owl swooped down he caught one rabbit by the haunch, a devoured sacrifice. Eleanor saw her words being written in the book made of the branch where he had launched. The owl finished his meal and emitted a screech of triumph. Eleanor felt the triumph resound through her body.

She was still awake at 3:00 am, listening to the silence of the backyard. She was like the owl, preying for the right language. She punctured the aura of all the disappointing men in her life. Not one man understood that she was who she was.

She no longer needed much, did not have to ask for the crutch of a fortune cookie message. Arthur had been right about that one thing, but he would never know the richness of her journey to arrive at the realization.

Alice called her from Chicago to say she was going to be married. It was Sam, a quiet guy she had met in college and had brought home several times. Mother and daughter were so happy to be who they were at that moment.

"Dad will be with us in spirit. Will you honor me by giving me away, Mom?"

"That would make me the happiest mom in the world."

Eleanor rode the bus down to Chicago for the ceremony. Cityscapes streamed by and placed her in a busy world, a haze of reflection on the face looking back at her. Kids these days, they were lucky to be just starting out. If their life was a carousel of possibility, hers was a beacon of words.

Eleanor hooked arms with Alice and walked her down the aisle. She felt the remembered glow of standing next to her eight-year-old daughter, arms spinning her around in a game of statue-maker. Freeze! Be a crouching tiger. A swooping owl. Make your life. On the ride home after the ceremony Eleanor began to write it all down in lyrics and symbols, straight to the truth, right there on the bus. By owl-light she fed the hunger of her language.

The Art of Comeback

Amy met her old lover walking down State Street arm in arm with some bespectacled woman. His red hair and beard had turned stark white. The years since the 1980s had changed her, too. As the decades passed, strong love for her now-departed husband George and their challenges with a strong-willed daughter had chiseled a fierceness upon her once-malleable face. She thought about a poem she was in the middle of writing about how your reactions allow you to make your own face. She used her startle to gather the courage to speak.

"Hi, Jim. I didn't know you were back in town. How's the West Coast?"

"Oh." He unarmed the woman and fumbled at his brief-case. "Hi, Amy. I'm in town for a Baseball in Literature conference. Keynote speaker. You know how I love the game. This is Trudy."

Trudy chirped "hi," stretched her arms, elbows out. Instead of offering a handshake, she merely rotated her shoulder muscles. Was she a passionate bird, camouflage specks on her clipped wings? When Jim said "love the game" he sounded as methodical and self-assured as he had all those years ago on Starkweather Creek. He was the embodiment of a true Irish mischief maker. Spin the spitball. Let me calculate my strategy.

She let him play it out. Or not. "I'd suggest a beer at Bob and Jean's, but they tore it down years ago in the name of progress."

He laughed. They shared the memory of those pitchers of beer and ardent literary discussions. Amy felt in her very being that the word "ardent" was just right. Ardor of her intensity and dent for the mark he had left in her heart.

"Would have loved that. But Trudy and I are running late. Have to make that keynote speech I told you about." His voice threw out that same Irish lilt. She wished she had heard it way back then. Sure 'n I'll be gone. Let me just brag about my game play.

She could see that this would be a brief encounter. No use arguing with the call. She watched Jim and Trudy, arms reattached, strutting away. The sight of their vanishing felt like the time he suddenly left, it had seemed like in the middle of the night, but maybe he had given her more of a warning than she could see at the time. It was only after he left that she learned to look for mute signs.

They had borrowed a neighbor's trailer and rowboat, launched at Starkweather Creek. The full moon directed them from the creek toward the lake, a beacon guiding them through milkweed wishes and cattails and algae. His steerage was off-kilter. The boat hit a rock and overturned. She laughed, swallowing a mouthful of dirty water. He cursed the gods who placed a rock in his way. Their swishing disturbed the mud, making the moon crease a wry smile upon the water. Pulling the boat back to the launch, they shimmied themselves up the slimy shore. Shoes squished toward the car. So much for moonlight serenades. The "s" sounds must have meant her life sucked. If she'd only listened.

That past memory faded, replaced by his white hair hovering above his absence. She continued her walk down State, searching for the hippie flair and the dedicated homeless window washer. High rises blocked her view. Too much gentrification. There were no good dive bars left. She stopped at a nameless outdoor table and ordered herself a beer in honor of her chance meeting with Jim.

She had missed him terribly those first few months. But then, since it was not meant to be, she began to miss him less. She searched her memory for the signs Jim might have left. Or was he just an intellectual cad? She thought of the time they went to a Milwaukee Brewers baseball game. They shared a beer out of a green-and-orange striped bucket. That was a sign of closeness, right? In retrospect a bucket was not a promising vessel for a relationship. Another time they took his father to a Brewers game. His thick Boston accent rattled around in her head. The impish Irish blood coursed through the beer in his father's cup. Do you really introduce a parent to someone you are only toying with? They laughed as they watched Bernie Brewer celebrate a homerun by sliding down the victory slide, stealing the catcher's mute gestures for the opposition's next play. Jim put a conspiratorial arm around his father. Together they made baseball into a strategy for living, learned how to play the steal game from Bernie's furtive look. Their eyes spit glee.

Amy sat at the outdoor table thinking about the game of baseball in a *The Art of Fielding* kind of way, the choreography of female and male ballet, poetry in motion. Just as in the novel there would come the inevitable slump. Art was all about comeback. The book hadn't spun into her heart until 2015, too late for discussion with George, too late to help her understand Jim.

The poetry of baseball had been grounded in her as far back as grade school when the nuns would let the squirmy kids listen to the occasional game over the loudspeaker. Those strict disciplinarians could be cruel with a rap of the ruler on disobeying knuckles, but they did love God and the Milwaukee Braves. The nuns used statistics and batting orders and strategy for the glory of learning.

In eighth grade the warring tug of her own Irish/English heritage stole her over to conniving puberty. She skipped out of school, took the city bus to Milwaukee County Stadium, used her babysitting money to purchase a cheap seat behind a pillar. "Pillar," another poetic word that meant exactly what it said. The sweet pill of naughtiness and the lair of a wild animal run home. Watching the Braves win was such fun! All she had to do was tell her Mom she was going to the library after school. Amy convinced herself that the nuns would appreciate her self-driven math lesson. She was too young to foresee that the nuns would call home. It was inevitable that her parents found out about her truancy. Then there was all hell to pay. For the first time of many she heard the words "you are campused" used as a form of punishment. She wasn't allowed to go anywhere for four whole months. When she was finally free school was back in session and Milwaukee was not in the playoffs.

As Amy looked back over her long relationship with the game, a hand touched her heart and spoke of baseball as the art of promise. Amy looked in her pocket mirror and saw etchings moving her face forward. Jim could wow his students, he could continue to strut his stuff out on the West Coast. She, Amy, would look from behind pillars to field her own words, catch quiet gestures of gratitude other people held in their hands. She finally understood that Jim's pitches had been wide of their mark all along, even though the lecture hall would continue to resound with applause. She got up from the table to continue walking. She read the signals in caught moments. Up ahead, that woman's hand cupped against her lips to increase the volume of her words was the spitting image of herself making an outstretched effort at speech. A comeback. She caught a laugh and spun it, moving with the spirit of George across fields of vision. The grass strummed again against her ankles and summoned up the rebellious girl in her. She felt the Irish and English vie for mastery. English decorum was losing out. Feral ancestry sprung from inside the lair of her poetry. She walked with urgency.

Driftwood

The little HUD apartment was just fine. The walls sloped at angles so Eleanor never did feel boxed in. Once she was satisfied with the new furniture arrangement, she made herself some tea. The kettle hummed on her stove then burst into a sharp-pitched whistle, stirring the air alive with the call for attention. She dressed the peppermint tea up with lemon and honey, then sunk into the only chair in the living room.

She breathed in the vapors, felt her nose clear, and with a raised cup said a momentary goodbye to the political world. She had been at a political rally and had been consumed by the need for urgent change. She had calmed herself by helping her next-door neighbor weed her garden. Now she needed a break. She glanced around her newly orchestrated book-filled room. The stained-glass parrot perched on the ceiling above the bookcase was swinging over a treasure on the top of the upper wood shelf: a single piece of driftwood.

Eleanor held the driftwood up toward the eye of the parrot, turning it so she could see all of the carvings the waves had wrought upon the wood. Her hands held eons of messages from the sea.

The piece of driftwood had spoken to Eleanor and her husband Ray when they were walking on the beach in Oregon those many years ago. Now that he was gone she brought it with her every time she moved around Madison.

If she held it close to her heart she could still feel the throb, the lover-come-back part of who they were.

She examined the two faces the waves had carved, one on each end, eyes etched above open mouths trying to talk. She was delighted to realize some new information just now coming into her mind. The wood told her it was an amphibian crawling on earth, giving birth to a young one pulsing in the water. The years of waves gave voice to her opening mouth in a half smile of achievement. The baby being born in the water smiled too, the crack at the end of her mouth turning upward, the antithesis of a human birth cry.

Eleanor held the amphibian close to her own face. The eye of the mother circled in a darker wood where the waves had lapped particularly lovingly. The darkest of all, the pupil at the center, looked past her, trying to focus on the big question: where are we going? Ray knew but hadn't told her yet. The nose of the mother breathed in possibility, a half parenthesis of space. The baby amphibian's dark circled eye looked to deeper water. It would take her gradual time to learn how to crawl upon the earth.

She poured more tea, raised her cup to her husband, above somewhere in a black hole. He was in a different form now, in a stratosphere of the human brain potential. Her hands held the driftwood tightly.

Eleanor felt the rotating facets of life, birth, death, evolution converge inside the water's artistry. Ray's pulse came back. The throb entered through the palms of her hands. She felt its steady beat in the fluid lapping of waves upon the Oregon shore. The Pacific Ocean continued to heave its messages. Driftwood crawled out of the water and new forms of being left footprints pointing forward in the sand.

The Union House Tavern

Louise felt that familiar lump. Her throat was parched from working the earth. Ahead was the only bar in town without ferns or chrome. She said goodbye to her vagabond friends, the ones who hung around to watch her garden, and went inside. The atmosphere was cool and dark, resplendent with the history of army boots on the floor railing and the raised glasses of relief from battle. Lives from training for long ago Civil War struggles returned to renew their vows. The bar was alive with the past. She read it in the crowd's lit faces.

She was glad for the anonymity. No one here knew her as the farmers market lady. She ordered a PBR to honor Wisconsin's past, raised her glass as in days of old. A wrinkled gentleman with a bow tie and a cocked fedora raised his beer glass in response. He looked to her like the blues man John Lee Hooker, calling up guttural sounds from another era. Louise couldn't help but smile. She'd been listening to a Blues-ology program on the radio. It was how she tuned in when she wanted to find the origins of rock and roll.

The jukebox was playing more innocent stuff, and right now she heard an oldies version of "Come Rain or Come Shine." She yearned to have a blues-man muddy it up. She thought the words held meaning for her. She needed both rain and sun for her garden and her life. She regarded her vegetables as individuals, groomed her red peppers and cabbage for extra crunch. She began to sway to the salsa of the tomato.

The fedora guy kept raising his glass toward her. Well, she knew she could groom him too. She moved over a barstool and sat closer. The guy's dark face moved like the flash of a bar sign. A whole dialogue occurred without talking. Suddenly he swept his hat off his head and bowed, a tipsy little gesture of respect. The beer in her throat was a gold rush.

"John" was in front of her, his arms danced around her. Other people in the bar clapped. The slicked back silver-headed bartender put his hand over her beer mug: "Behave." Hold on. Tighten up. Instead Louise and the bow tie danced, they swooped low. She understood that the man was giving her a writhing motion, a half century worth of experience. Just like the street people, the bartender, some new guy she'd never seen before was going to have to put up with her defiance.

Out of the corner of her eye she spied Rip. She had thought he was still down south. She saw a stab of jealousy written on his face. She danced her way toward him. John Lee Hooker followed. She couldn't help but be happy to see Rip.

"Welcome back. Ain't life grand?"

She thought of their past together. He was always striking out for new places like some damn wealthy snowbird. She stirred the waters by flirting with both men, the flicker of her eyelashes like a neon sign. The bartender's worried face backed off. This flirty banter was just barroom lingo. John pulled at his fedora and slid back to his bar stool. She patted the stool next to her and invited Rip over. She beamed her gladness to see her traveling man, knowing that the way to love was to set her man free. Then blues-men would want to get back home.

Rip touched her face.

"Mr. Bojangles decided to stay down south a little while longer. I knew I had to come back. I need to be in your zone." Just like the John Lee Hooker song said!

His eyes studied her like he couldn't get enough. "I'm with you always." She loved the way he talked. His voice held a wedge against her heart. She too felt zoned.

The Bubbler

For Rita Mae Reese

Amy quenched her thirst for knowledge by roaming the isthmus in her city. She always walked around the Bubbler at the Central Library looking for engaging literary events. She loved the good old-fashioned slang of "bubbler" for drinking fountain. People could appreciate the creativity of the water flow. The Bubbler announced that local poet Rita Mae Reese was giving a reading the next evening from her work in progress. Not published yet, but these new poems would become part of her lexicon. The word "progress" caught Amy's attention because she felt her entire life was like that. An unfolding. She never could sit still, as Emily Post said ladies should do. She had long ago shed the white gloves and raised pinkie finger.

It was difficult to drive at night. The street lights sometimes doubled the lane she should be driving in. She squirted an extra dose of Visine in to correct the tendency and started for the library. A young policeman pulled her over. She thought she had been driving fine. The swirling red and blue lights on the top of his squad car emphasized the seriousness on his face. Oh. Her license plate renewal. She was driving okay. Her plate had expired. She could offer proof that she was not a criminal. Her glove compartment (cars still had such a thing!) contained her proof of registration. She had paid her dues, had merely been waiting to get to a car wash before sticking the new expiration date on her plate. The cop let her go. Would he have done the same for a Black driver? For her daughter Gwen?

Amy walked into the library feeling like she had been sprung from jail. No matter what the poet was working on her progression of words would be inspirational. The room was sparsely populated. Many people still didn't understand how poetry could illuminate who they were becoming. She settled herself in a nearby chair, hand thrust inside her pocket to make sure she had brought along the eye drops for the drive home.

The poet was pale, with a long-drawn face and wet eyes. She began to speak about post-election blues. Her voice had a bit of a croak in it, a frog struggling to retain her green life. Amy wanted to nourish her from the nearby bubbler, revive her with good old Wisconsin slang. The poet spoke a poem about racial tension, how the alt-right was already making it worse. Her words grasped the agony of the Madison mother whose young, Black, unarmed son had been shot dead by a policeman. The air in their city was ripe with the stench of strange fruit. Amy smelled it on the news every night. The poet was refusing to let the stench go. She spoke her progression through grinding teeth. Then it was too much for her. She burst into sobs, right there in the middle of the reading. Amy rushed to bring her a cup of water from the bubbler. The poet took a gulp and brought herself back together.

She said to the room: "Hung from trees with white sheets."

Amy glanced at the entranced woman sitting near her. She stretched out her arms as if to embrace both the poet and the woman. "Rita Mae's words are all the more powerful for being graphic." The woman nodded in agreement. They shook hands, vowed to speak up, work to stop the killing of young Blacks innocently eating candy bars. Hung just the same as yesterday's strange fruit. You need to cry out.

They stopped to thank Rita Mae for her reading and buy the poetry book she had already published. Amy looked at the poet's freshly inked inscription: "For Amy, in appreciation for understanding that thin skin is sometimes necessary to get the word out."

The next morning Amy took herself to the zoo. There, still on the central pathway, was the big round stone bubbler she had taken her daughter to all those years ago. She had watched Gwen climb onto the circular stone steps and lean in for a drink. Now she sat on a nearby bench and, with the black stripes of tigers and the dark roar of lions in the background, she watched sweet little feet climb the stone steps. Amy watched faces of many hues lean in to slurp a drink. The young mother and daughter sitting next to her on the bench sharing Skittles laughed in the flow of water as it touched many children's lips. The daughter jumped down to add her dark brown face to the mix. Her wide lips brought the exact image of six-year-old Gwen leaning into the bubbler. She held on to a fierce cry that her daughter would stay safe.

Bittersweet

The senior citizens in low-income housing projects deserved to keep their dignity. Once a week a bus picked them up and took them to a local restaurant for an actual order-from-the-menu breakfast. Maddy helped facilitate the group, explaining choices, taking names, providing the support of her arm to a person in pain. They paid by donation.

She had continued to volunteer at the meal sites after Stuart left her. She needed to keep her own dignity too, surface from the drowning feeling. She especially liked restaurant day because there was a fireplace she could stare into.

The waitresses were so kind, always calling Maddy and the older folk "dear" or "sweetie," always remembering to bring ketchup for their potatoes. Butter for their toast. Lemons for their ice water. They would offer a small bowl of fresh strawberries, grapes, tangerine slices to each guest. After the meal the waitresses placed a single piece of dark chocolate in front of everyone. Most saved the chocolate for later, but Maddy always ate hers right away. She savored the feel of the dark chocolate in her mouth. She would look into the blue and red burning flames of the fire and slow down the swallow of the treat. She had gotten accustomed to the stronger flavor. The taste always felt like the flames of her life.

When Stuart had left she went crazy for a while, and no dose of dark chocolate could ease the pain. Bursts of song helped bring her around, followed by bursts of flavor. She lingered in front of the fireplace, entranced by the dance of dark and fire. She was beginning to ignite her own life again. The spark came from within, not some outside source.

On their bus ride back to senior housing, she digested the fuel of the morning. The senior citizens were bouncing in their seats, chattering like grade schoolers. There were no boundaries. She felt the gulp of change in her throat. She closed her eyes and the flames flickered higher. A song was in order. The seniors liked it when she initiated a melody.

"Row, Row, Row Your Boat . . ."

She was saving herself from drowning. Craggy voices burst into song. The old nursery rhyme echoed in the canyon of the yellow school bus. Voices paced themselves at intervals for choral unison. Maddy repeated the words, the fire within now a gentle outstretched glow of embers. She relished the attention to their dignity. The good thing about singing with these folks was that everyone rowed along. They knew what she was talking about. When life hands you tangerines, shake a tambourine.

Troubled Eyes

For the first time in their friendship Eleanor and Amy had to make a genuine effort at dialogue. The election results had been shocking. Instead of shouting in the streets people were holed up behind the closed doors of their grief. Eleanor had finally ventured out to test the extent of the damage done, knocking ever so lightly on Amy's apartment door. Her friend cracked the door open as far as the chain on the bolt would allow. All Eleanor could see were her large, welled-up eyes. She recognized her own hurt reflected back at her. They were both taking the triumph of the right wing hard.

"Can you let me in so we can talk?"

Amy slowly unbolted the chain and let her friend in. The two women hugged. Eleanor felt abrasions of Amy's thin skin rub against her own thicker skin, different exposures of grief and healing. Eleanor's failed relationships with men had forged an armor of protection against onslaught. Amy marched thin-skinned across her raised fist of a life, radicalized but sensitive like the poetry residing inside their friendship. Before either could speak further Amy gave an involuntary sob from some deep cavern within. She regained her composure with firm declarative sentences.

"I'm moving to Canada. The weather is much the same, thanks to global warming. The alt-right hierarchy will make everything dangerously worse."

Eleanor settled herself directly across from Amy's favorite chair. She was prepared to begin their effort at speech. She owned her words:

"The truth of the matter: we have to stay and make it better."

"How can we possibly have any effect on Washington? They don't understand that, looking back, we are all immigrants. We all must now live in the ghetto of right-wing choices."

Eleanor leaned into the cushioned comfort of her chair. How could she explain to Amy that to run away was a placid act in a tumultuous time? They must balance themselves on the ridge of the housing projects and fight.

"You are free to choose and that in itself is a blessing. Gwen has flown the nest and will make her own choices. But does Canada even want a bunch of disgruntled new citizens? Better to stay here and make small gestures toward change. Speak to me. Tell me what you are thinking ..."

Amy stood and reached across the empty space between them. She allowed her fingertips to touch Eleanor's lips.

"Every time we talk I see you grow to know me more. That is a blessing. But this election travesty seems more than I can bear. Booted out immigrants. Economic disparity. Racial profiling. No Black person can wear a hoodie and sunglasses without being in danger. No one should get in a car. I'm afraid for my daughter."

Eleanor looked out at the leaves falling from the dark November sky. The once colorful fluttering crinkled and withered on the vine.

"The weather is extreme. Across the nation we have either drought or deluge. Fires rage. The earth cracks. The winter vortex is new to my vocabulary. Listen. Noisy unnecessary leaf blowers invade people's space.

"The country needs a good old-fashioned sweeping. We can be the people who get it done, like those blacklisted artists whose stance helped to sweep away McCarthyism ..."

Eleanor saw the well of fears in Amy's eyes overflow. They both sat in the small sanctuary of the apartment looking at the fears, as if examining all possibilities. The effort at speech had become internal. Try to go clear. Reach me. Join hands. Sweep.

They rose up to hug each other. Amy showed Eleanor to the door, sighing.

"I'll think about what you said. Canada still calls me."

Eleanor retreated back to the safety of her own apartment. She ignored all news outlets for the rest of the day, insisting on her own savage peace. At night she emailed Amy what she hoped was a consoling message, straight from her heart.

Dear Amy,

I saw the well of tears in your eyes today. I'm writing to you to see if you're better. I don't think the answer is to move to a different country. Besides, no country wants to accept the vast majority of upset people. Studying the California results would be a sane place to begin. Reform at the state level, work to transform our rural Wisconsin voters. Go to those northern diners and bars, the places where locals blurt out their opinions.

I remember how you told me you changed peoples' minds at that Norske Nook in Osseo. You had toddler Gwen in tow to visit family further north. She was the only Black person in that town. The heads in the diner turned in frowning unison. You heard a bearded woodsman mutter: "Why don't people stick with their own kind?" You told me his words were a strangle on your very effort to breathe. "Kind" was the operative word. You and Gwen smiled a gentle greeting in reply and exhaled through the "My Favorite Things" song. People perked up upon hearing the familiar lyrics.

Gwen broke into her famous Sesame Street dance. You both quickly held their spinning minds in your cupped palms. Supplication. The woodsman huffed, never convinced of your need to breathe, got on his Harley and roared away. The rest of the townspeople smiled their cautious smiles. One little old lady said "thank you for making my day." The busy waitress called you "darlin's" and gave you an especially generous piece of their famous pie.

So let me remind you that the smallest of gestures matters. We learned about small gestures the first time we met at the demonstration on Willy Street. We are in the world to change the world. You and Gwen are where you need to be. I know your sorrow has no sense of time: we have four years to get our message across, to travel across Wisconsin and get to know people.

I hope that as you reflect on the devastating results of the election your mind becomes clear.

Love, Eleanor

The days passed in disarray. Then she got a brief e-mail reply from Amy that spoke volumes:

I'm planning a trip up to northern Wisconsin next week before the first snow hits. Ready for coffee and fish specials and pie. Would you like to come along?

Collection Redemption

Amy was taking her daily walk along tree-lined streets with no sidewalks. She heard a clunker of a bicycle coming up behind her. The rattletrap of used parts clacked against each other and suddenly stopped. She turned around and watched an older guy lean down to examine an object in a driveway. Trash collection fodder. He put the bag of who-knew-what in his bicycle basket and continued on his way in her direction.

Amy couldn't help but be curious. "Find a new treasure?"

The guy broke into the most disarming smile. His laugh lines furrowed upward and his green eyes sparked a quest. He stopped his bike in front of her and opened the newly found bag. Bottle caps of many hues smiled back. Amy reached into the bag to examine several of the bottle caps more closely. She fingered the rough edges. It dawned on her that the consumer of the bottles must be a local craft beer lover. She now knew which block to stroll on for her craft beer education.

The guy too reached into the bag. When he held the caps up in the sunlight he marveled at the variety of colors. "Wow. Listen to these names flourishing on the caps. 'Gold Rush.' 'Unbridled.' God's Nectar.' 'Toga Party.' 'Big Lebrewski!'" Amy had to adjust her glasses to see the small letters on the Lebrewski cap. When he held up another one "Orion!" she witnessed stars flashing in the sunlight.

She reached back into the bag and felt the wealth of colors and words as she would in a found stash of coins. This neighbor had apparently been experimenting with many different brands. The collector introduced himself as Mark and walked along with her, the aged bicycle rolling beside him. He was recently retired, new to the neighborhood. He was an artist, he explained, and would listen to what the bottle caps told him. Sometimes it would take a while for the found object to speak. His new apartment was already cluttered. He would have to use a forest outside the city limits to hold all his valuables, and would somehow have to keep the forest pristine.

They stopped in front of the Little Free Library perched on a mail post smack dab in the middle of the block. Mark chose *The Professor and The Madman*. A quick glance at the subtitle told Amy something about this new man: "The Making of the Oxford English Dictionary." Another word person! The neighborhood was getting more interesting. He slipped the book into his basket.

They resumed their walk. A man was hauling something big to the end of his driveway. It looked like part of a barn floor that had been scuffed and varnished and re-scuffed. The well-worn polka dance of life. Mark expressed interest in the piece. "I could carve this wood floor into many pieces, shape many useful objects." The man said "Free. U-Haul." When he saw the old man shrug he amended his message. "Or, for twenty bucks I can drop it off." Mark's face lit up all over again. Amy handed him a pen from the dentist office and he quickly wrote down his address. She had gotten the pen when the kind dentist had put the confidence back in her smile. Mark shoved off to meet the man at his apartment.

She watched him pedal hurriedly away. The clunking noises faded. She wondered where he would put that big piece of wood. What would the worn slats say? She walked over to the local public library and checked out the book about the Oxford English Dictionary. She liked thinking she and Mark would be reading the same book at the same time. New words were always being added, yet there was comfort in the original words that began being gathered in 1857 and took seventy years to complete. Sure, she could argue against the patriarchal Victorian tone. But she would let her own word choices liberate the language, free the definitions from the prison of a stringent moral code. She had a burning desire to read her short stories to Mark. She hadn't had time to note his address. Chance had brought them together and chance would have to orchestrate a reunion.

The next week she took a walk on a new route through the Aldo Leopold Nature Conservancy. She respected the bear mound and walked around it, not over it. Native American voices drummed their support. From way in the distance she saw a rusty bicycle seat thrusting up, parting the grass. Upon closer inspection she thought it looked like the bike she saw Mark with the other day. She passed the bike, walked on to a small pond and found Mark bending over to look in the tall grass. He shook cattails near their roots. The seat of his pants shaped the curves of his bottom. She had a proclivity for just such an ass.

Mark straightened up. He did not appear surprised at all to see her. His smile reached her heart and his eyes glistened pond light. "The cattails may enhance my gathering of pussy willows. My two ancient cats will be so pleased to bat them around. I am now on the prowl for some kind of receptacle to hold them loose and free for soft paws."

Amy was totally allergic to cats. She was disappointed to be unable to visit his new apartment, wherever it may be.

"Would you like to start walking together every day? Or maybe several times a week? I don't own a bike, so you may need more time to scavenge."

And so it began in earnest, Mark looking for found objects and Amy searching for the words that would free her language. Mark found her a creaky bicycle and that helped the search. During their spins in the neighborhood he would tell her a little about himself. She cringed when he talked about his ex-wife, who still seemed to be an important part of his life. The ex furnished him with herbal tea and helped store his growing art collection. To make her voice equal, Amy told Mark about losing her husband George. It was a subject she hardly ever broached, a necessary revelation to a person she cared about. Mark listened intently, his eyes reaching out to envelop her, a redemptive rag man drawing circles around her heart.

They found a broken stained-glass window ready for pickup. Mark said it was meant to hold the dried cattails and pussy willows. He glued the colored glass together to form a vase and told Amy he placed his newly created object in a sunny spot where the cats loved to lounge. When the sun began to set the glass threw colors of light upon all the art on his walls.

Amy wished she could see the vase, see the art on the colors moving across the walls. She would never be able to go near his apartment, never be near his cats.

Later that year, when they had gotten to know each other very well indeed, Mark brought the vase over for her to see the colors gliding across her own walls. They watched the subtle spectacle together. Then he presented Amy with a star necklace, a constellation of words made of bottle caps housed in a small box he had created from the dance of wooden slats.

Lunate Bone

Amy watched the dog food commercial, the one where the wolf transformed into a small dog. The wolf in the commercial joined his pack and ran off. Her husband George had done the same, joining his union activities from a sky-view. When she lost her little old dog after George's death, she couldn't bring herself to replace the absence of either. That was her excuse for sitting paralyzed in front of the TV.

She turned the TV off. Her mind began to work again. She knew that all creatures, human, animal, insect, reptile, held their ancestors within. The very bones of her being whistled ancient messages of survival. After all these years she was still searching for the light to shine on her voices from the past, way back to the origins of us all. Maybe the eyes of a dog could teach her.

She forced herself to go to the pound. For years she had avoided the Humane Society headquarters; she didn't trust herself to withstand each and every dog. She knew she would look into their eyes and want to rescue everyone. The reality was that a no-kill pound did not exist. Even an eighty percent successful adoption rate was too low. How could she get beyond the pleading eyes of the incarcerated? That recent transformative dog food commercial told her it was time to embrace her nature, choose a dog.

The volunteer behind the desk offered to take her down the rows of caged animals. There was whimpering and the smell of urine. Amy wondered if she could make herself do this death row walk. The volunteer was kind and reached out to comfort each grateful dog.

"There is a short history on most of these dogs if you are interested . . ."

Amy was surprised by her matter-of-fact tone. Then again the woman was probably here many hours a week. She must have shielded herself from the euthanasia aspect of the pound.

Most dogs had their noses as far out of the cage as possible, begging. One had curled herself in a back corner, nose hidden under her paws, resigned. Amy chose that little gal. She seemed the wisest of them all. The volunteer pursed her lips, coaxing the dog to the front of her cage.

"There is no history on this dog. No name tag. No way of knowing much about her. She is a healthy stray, about five years old. Came to us un-spayed. No one has paid much attention to her."

The nameless dog looked right through Amy. Her eyes were full moons. Amy scratched her behind her ears, named her Luna. Luna was some kind of rat terrier/beagle mix. Good. Mutts lived longer than the aristocratic. All those different ancestors howled for attention.

She walked Luna to make sure they were a good fit. The dog's black, brown, and white coat glimmered in the tall grass. Luna showed restraint, didn't tug at her leash at all. She would be manageable for Amy's wobbly gait. On the car ride home the dog sat as close to Amy as possible, next to her but not on top of her. Respect. She seemed to enjoy the car ride.

Once home Luna investigated every inch of the small apartment, then jumped up on the couch to be near Amy. Her eyes looked distant yet longing, as if she had much to say. It was not too soon to listen. The dog held her ancestors' experiences in her eyes. Amy saw echoes of survival. Luna opened up the passageway so that Amy's human ancestors came out swinging.

The Irish ancestors cleared away the littered trail of her George's death. Dear George, in that howl of a wolf laugh, told her to move on. He was a throbbing presence. Amy heard him through the lunate bone of her wrist. She put down food and water in a raised double-sided bowl. Luna wolfed down her dinner. She gave the dog a small rawhide bone as a welcome home treat. Amy heard the whistling of her own bones.

Before sleep she pulled the curtain back to watch the sliver of the moon begin a new journey. The moon possessed a probing quality, as if every punctuation would contain an answer. George's sky-view.

That night Luna slept in Amy's arms, nose pressed into her wrist, taking her pulse.

Survival

He had invited her to a hazy restaurant near the water's edge; the foghorns were blaring warnings. Her heart pounded in her ears. The items on the menu sounded less than enticing: Rack of lamb, a torture; stewed rabbit, poor little dear; a hashish of prunes, Maddy's intestines quaked. The man sitting across from her seemed to be punishing her on purpose. Her intuition told her that he was only there out of some misplaced sense of duty. He had used her all up like doodles on a crumpled piece of paper. She was a mere linear drawing in his scheme of things, the stick figure of a praying mantis hobbled to the twig of her discontent, an inch away from any useful prayer. And yet he would never admit to seeing her that way. She knew he felt uneasy because he did not like metaphors, mistrusted the play of language. She could see his enthusiasm for her way of seeing had waned by the stare of his eyes. The song that went through her head was the same one endeared by Vietnam vets everywhere: "We Gotta Get Out of This Place." The Animals knew how to escape.

Maddy looked at the entrenched man through the lowered barrier of the menu. His face was as still as a statue. The heart was missing from the table. She pushed her chair back and stood. She was in no way hungry. A leave-taking was essential.

"I need to ramble on back home. Got a dog to feed, words to read, and raw lyrics to cup in my hands. Feed my soul to the flock of sheep . . . It's been real." She liked the startle of his eyes as she inched away from the gristle of the scene.

Gulps of newly crisp air helped cleanse her insides. Maddy knew in the depths of her being that it was better to be alone and began walking the miles back to her apartment. The setting sun shone a red-veined spotlight upon the changing neighborhoods. She saw the faces of strangers illuminate the streets and merged herself among the anonymous. An old flea market loomed ahead, a marvel of used goods, a carnival of junk, heaps of flannel shirts and children's worn out toys that someday just had to go. She held up a discarded toy for further inspection: Someone had loved that well-worn bear once and he would be loved again. He was stronger for his missing nubs of fur. The sound of bargaining voices clamored windfall deals. Warped fun house mirrors distorted and uncovered her face, making her ask the question: "Who are you?" Maddy became aware of the lop-sided look on her lips. Would she ever eat lamb at Easter? Maybe she would become a vegetarian. A can of kidney beans was starting to sound good. She felt lost in the maze of fun house mirrors. She was too fat, then she was too skinny. She couldn't seem to find her way out. She backed away and became aware of the changing lift of her needs. Her mouth was restored to speech. It made her ask this question: Besides dead meat was there anything she needed to be rid of?

That clunky chaise lounge came to mind. It was too deep and she was finding it harder and harder to climb out of it. She wanted to put a bookcase in its place.

The people running the flea market said they would sell it for her if she could get it to them. She tried to think of someone who might help her. She walked the rest of the way home going through the mental file of disappointing men. Little Fydo greeted her excitedly at the door. She loved literature and had proudly named her little guy Fydo Dogstoyevsky.

A complication entered her mind. Fydo was dexterous and really appreciated that old chaise lounge. He hopped on it now, hoping to get close to her height. She scratched and soothed her dog. The apartment held her in comforting arms.

Maddy had purchased the chaise lounge five years earlier, after Stuart had left her. She remembered his blank stare, as prominent in her mind as the look on this evening's dinner companion's face. His exact words: "My bags are packed." With Stuart she had felt so alone and the chair wrapped itself around her, right there in the furniture store. Three Men and a Truck had moved it from her old house to her new apartment.

Now it was time to contemplate something new. Maddy joined Fydo on the chair, sinking down into the cushioned morass. When she held her dog she felt her own heartbeat. The chaise lounge would need to stay. It was stronger than the disappointing men. With Fydo's help she would inch her way out again. He would need canned meat, slurps of water. He would need to be brought outside and walked. The chaise lounge was all the world to her; she would find a way to inch herself free. Fydo licked her face and the carnival of distortion went away.

Gate

Mark the Collector had taken a hiatus. Amy missed seeing him ride his bike through the neighborhood. Perhaps he had found an object he got so involved with that he had flown away in its grasp: transported. It was easy for an artist to put more effort into art than into relationships. Amy knew instinctively that she had to let him go. She was getting older and must release the disappointments. Her treasured memories were with her forever. Husband George, now deceased. Daughter Gwen. Friends Eleanor and Maddy. She set out to look for these people's spirits in her own collection journeys.

She still had the creaky bicycle Mark had welded together for her. She chuckled out loud. She had transformed herself into a babushka-wearing old lady clacking around the neighborhood, taking one hand off the handlebar to constantly adjust thick eyeglasses across the bridge of her nose. She used the glasses like binoculars, spying for objects that she might turn into words. Words built bridges, an architecture of connection.

The heat of late summer brought living, breathing things. At the edge of the city she heard the companionship of wolves howl their unisons of longing. Her very throat joined the clamor. She remembered one of George's habitual declarations. He would tip his hat and say "go howl yourself at the moon." People would look at him: "what?" George lived life around a primitive campfire. He liked to take a branch, stir the embers. She remembered times when he would tell a tale of a wolf communicating with the fullness of the moon. He gestured into the embers and said: "The wolf has all the power. Open the gates. Just say what you hear." She understood his storytelling more than most and in that sense the sound of wolves brought him to her.

On a bike ride closer to her apartment the flutter of wings inspired her. But she never had it in her heart to net a butterfly, study the colors as an object. She remembered how, as a young girl, she had read about the migration of monarchs. The memory spoke to her. Amy was a person who planted milkweed, then let the butterflies go on their courageous journey to the mountains of Mexico. They pollinated the earth along the way. Pollinators were in her yard, never to be pinned down. Dragonflies announced their probing presence. They would linger in front of her, their beating rainbow wings conveying vast benefits, then speed on, clearing away the destructive mosquitos.

Near the cattails next to the pond she spied the shed skin of a garden snake. Amy stooped to handle the scaly object. The molt spoke growth, renewed life. An object could hold the power of rebirth. She shivered and returned the snakeskin to its resting place. She kept shivering in the heat of this summer day because she was going to have to work through some pain. The cattails reminded her of Mark, her vanished Collector, him leaning over in the tall grass to look for treasures. And the snakeskin reminded her of Gwen's wedding guest, the one who danced to Bruno Mars in snakeskin boots he bragged he bought in Portugal. He displayed his boots like a snake charmer trying to woo women. Amy laughed as she remembered how she, Eleanor, and Maddy had seen right through him. The friends danced to their own beat. She picked up the snakeskin again and placed it in her bicycle basket. She would mail it to Gwen and remind her of that charmer guest. Her daughter had learned from an early age to listen to what animals say. What kind of mother sends her daughter a molted snakeskin? Amy claimed herself to be that person. She could see Gwen's long piano fingers raise up in delight when she opened her gift box. Her own stubby fingers had wrapped it lovingly.

She clacked away from the memory of the wedding on her cobbled bicycle. Her binocular vision found an especially long and lush blade of grass and scooped it up in a clump of nourishing earth for Eleanor. It was the perfect wand to conduct her friend's affinity with Walt Whitman. She found a tassel of wild raspberries and picked some for Maddy to soothe the ache in her friend's troubadour throat. She wanted to make sure it was a taste that would help Maddy come out of herself. Amy chewed the sweet raspberry, felt the nubby seeds as they slid comfortingly down her throat.

The molten snakeskin, lush blade of grass, and wild raspberries brimmed through the bamboo of her bike basket. Her words wove a bramble of raspberries arching over tall blades of grass. A newly molted snake coiled around the gate. Riding with her was a voice slipping open the latch of a howl.

Wolf Moon

Amy rode her bicycle to a protected nature park and got off the suggested trail. Remnants of effigy mounds pointed to the pond. The cattails were bending down in supplication to the coming winter. She rode respectfully around the Native American Bear Mound to the little stream that fed into the pond. All of nature was getting ready for the harsh days ahead, just as she had folded into ground zero at the time of George's death. Amy sensed the change in seasons and decided to exchange her babushka for the orange-and-black matching hat and mittens, the ones Gwen had knit her for her birthday.

The following day dawned cold and she got her wool hat out for the new season. She fingered Gwen's choice of yarns. When she closed her eyes she saw orange and black streaking through the sky. She witnessed monarchs perching on effigy mounds and then migrating, landing on their Mexican mountain. Then she looked deeper and felt George's comforting arm hold her in the lap of the mountain, in the middle of his rise to new heights. He had the powerful ability to be with her even when he was long gone, the slant of his life snuffed out too soon.

She reached down to let pond water comfort her. It was even colder than a few days before, but not frozen yet. She leaned her bicycle against a tree stump and looked closely at the stream as it entered the pond. The movement of the water caressed a small stone. She knelt to pick up the object, her hand baptized by the tingle of cold. The stone glistened with red, black, and orange veins. She vowed to carry this found treasure in her pocket and finger it through all kinds of weather. Nature's rosary.

Onslaughts of colder weather pierced her breath. In January she went outside her apartment to view the full moon, the one Native Americans called the Wolf Moon. George howled from the lap of the mountain. Amy felt the little stone inside the mitten of her right palm. The color pattern whispered through the veins of her own skin. She held her monarch stone up to the moon. A breath of life could be in anything, even a little stone being polished in the middle of a stream.

River

Maddy went to Noah's Ark pet store on the northeast side of Madison to cuddle the animals at play. Holding the creatures quickly became too much. She had lost her dear dog Fydo and was still in grief. Then she saw the fish swimming in their aquariums. Freedom! In the store all the bettas were swimming in circles in small glass bowls. Watching them made her dizzy. On a lonely whim she purchased a betta fish. She also bought a larger aquarium. She knew immediately she would name her fish Vincent for van Gogh's magnificent palette of colors. Once ensconced in her apartment he seemed much happier, his purple, blue, and red body streaking back and forth looking for a fight. People had to let bettas live alone because no one could trust their personalities. The males killed each other off. All Vincent had to combat was his own reflection. When he saw himself his fins would rise up in even more colorful fury until he was satisfied in his victory. Maddy decided to move the aquarium to her dresser. It was higher up and she could better view his territorial glory. She re-filled it, purified it, and watched Vincent fight with himself throughout the day. He was the last thing she saw before sleep.

One morning the telephone rang earlier than usual. It was her neighbor La Verne asking if she would like to attend an event at the Senior Center. In a sleepy voice Maddy agreed to go. The center was always sponsoring interesting lectures and literary readings. La Verne promised to call and sign them both up for the event.

It wasn't until later in the day, when she was fully awake, that Maddy realized what she had gotten herself into. She went online to read the Senior Messenger and found out that the event La Verne was talking about was "Speed Dating for Senior Citizens." From the title alone Maddy had huge doubts about attending. She had avoided Match.com and all those other dating sites. No way would she ever trust internet strangers. And her experience with wayward old lover Stuart told her to mistrust in-person contacts as well. She could still feel the depth of the pain he had caused. She envisioned herself at the Senior Center, playing musical chairs, going from table to table, trying to charm the few available men. She never made a good first impression. She knew she would go down in defeat. And yet, there was a huge gap in her life. That night before sleep she watched Vincent swimming in majestic glory. She vowed to be like him, to protect the territory of her own well-being.

In the morning she awoke determined to call La Verne and cancel. She got out of bed and went over to get her first colorful sight of betta for the day. To her horror Vincent lay limp on the bedroom floor. She reached down to gather him up, carried him lifeless back to his tank, as if the gesture might rescue him. She must have filled the water too high and he swam into flight. She sighed. She always destroyed what she grew to love. When she closed her eyes she could see him over and over again flinging himself into the starry night sky.

At breakfast her hands were shaking. She spilled orange juice all over herself. She was drowning in her own breaths of air. When La Verne called to remind her about their afternoon appointment at the Senior Center she let the call go to her answering machine. She felt too paralyzed to even pick up the phone. The excited voice said "meet you in the Speed Dating Room at 2:30."

At 2:00 Maddy felt herself to be on automatic. She had emptied the aquarium, placing Vincent's body in a little box to be returned to the water when the weather got warmer. She had cleaned off the orange juice and put on her favorite purple, blue and red sweater, a winter memorial to her lost Vincent. Now the gap in her life was even wider. She felt the trench of burial pound in her heart. It would remain there for the months it would take the stream to thaw.

Maybe a trip to the Senior Center was a good idea. The distraction of a new person might free her from her self-imposed prison. On her way out to her car she saw her neighbor Harry coming through the door with his bicycle. He had on his usual baseball cap, a big Brewers fan even in the winter weather. He tipped the brim of his cap in her direction. "This cold air makes me anticipate Spring Training!" She admired his positive attitude. Sometimes he even took his dog on a romp, leash tied to his handlebars. They smiled at each other.

When she grabbed the safety bar to pull herself into her car she felt a surge of determination. Maybe she could be as free as Vincent had been for his brief moment in time. The engine idled; she tried to shake away the bleak winter day. Peeking in the rearview mirror, all determination left her. Deep grief was etched in the furrow of her casket brow. She pleaded out loud: "Don't let the senior citizens read this horrible day on my face." Too much emotional information was exposed in her look. She tried to gather strength, switched on the radio for company.

After some low watt static the voice of Joni Mitchell came on strong. She was looking for a river to skate away her pain. Maddy remembered that years ago she heard Joni Mitchell in person. Her pure voice and words had filled the entire Dane County Coliseum. Back then she had held the newspaper in her hands and learned that Joni was staying at the Edgewater Hotel. For a break from the music she had gone skating on Lake Mendota. Somewhere in Maddy's jumble of photographs sat a picture of Joni ice-skating in Madison on a frigid mysterious day.

Joni showed her appreciation to the city by choosing the skating scene for an album cover. Maddy listened intently to the song's words. "River" was all about despondency, the giving up of a child at birth, loss of relationships, yet the artist had found a way out. Madison gave her the icy depths she could use to get away from emotional turmoil. Maddy convinced herself to follow the lyrical example, purge her own losses. Instead of going to the Senior Center she drove to the nearby Yahara, walked the path along the frozen length of the river from Lakes Monona to Mendota and back. She taught herself freedom with every invigorating step. She began a slow jog next to the river. Now faster, so her hair rose up from under her wool hat, battling for possession of her face. The landscape spoke to her. Like Vincent she could streak across the water. She could fly. She was free to skate away in a blaze of cold blue sky.

The sun set upon a dab of red. Maddy got back in the car for the drive home. Vincent's colors etched her mind. At the entrance to the security locked apartment building she fumbled for her key, found it, buzzed herself in. Standing there was Harry, blue Brewers cap in his hands, looking like he had been waiting for her. For the first time she noticed his balding hair, the gap in his teeth, and the wonder in his eyes.

Grandad Bluff

Amy wondered how long Mark would stay in Madison. She reached for her heavy jacket to guard against onslaughts of cold air. Her newly rescued dog Luna immediately sensed something was up: "Include me! Please include me!!" In a calm voice she reassured Luna that she would return. She hoped the dog didn't yowl with separation anxiety while she was gone. She gave Luna some scratches behind her ears, left to meet her ex. He was out riding his bike, collecting treasures in her neighborhood. She would need the jacket as protection against the chill of his probable departure.

Mark looked older; his hair and beard were bushy white. She watched his beard raise up in the wind as he clackety-clacked his bike toward her. He stopped, leaned into her, drew out of his basket a photograph he had taken of a bluff along the Mississippi. Amy studied the photograph, noticed the faces coming out of the rocks, the worn carvings of ancient architecture. Indigenous people seemed to be looking down from the top of the bluff into the moving water below. The photograph swept Amy back to the power of the past. She could feel the craggy surfaces building toward crescendo.

Back when they were seeing each other as lovers she had told Mark all about being born in La Crosse, spending summers on her grandparents' Sky Hi Ranch, a young girl's paradise located right at the spine on top of Grandad Bluff. He knew her background and made his photograph of Grandad Bluff a gift. She remembered how he had found that place in her, they had done the love good, and he had held her, slipped back inside her with his words. It made her love him more. He had grown up in Trempealeau, another kid exploratory region right on the Mississippi. They had never met each other until the world considered them "old." They stood together leaning against their bikes and fingered the beauty of the bluff.

"I remember the full moon coming up above the ranch on the top of the bluff. As a girl I noticed it as a yellow glow over the uneven terrain." She told Mark how the horses would get spooked by the bright night and run up to the barn along the narrow trail, manes and tails flying. It was as if they were trying to reach the moon. Sinbad was always the leader of the pack. Oh, how her grandma hated that name. But Amy thought "Sinbad" was perfect to honor the horses who came before. The horse had a solid flight instinct, knew he had to break free in the race for survival. The old farm dogs Hoop and Sox would howl approval. The moon threw a spotlight on the gift the river had carved.

Mark's finger touched her face. "I'm going to go back and take more photographs, look from all angles, try to capture the vastness of the place. You deserve more gifts."

Mark had a certain aura that came through his art, be it photography or frames of found objects from nature. He had gone off alone for a few years to live in a cabin in the woods near Perrot State Park and work on his assemblages of forms. The move made them friends instead of lovers. The bottle caps in Madison were replaced by his backwoods scavenge for the fossil imprints on rocks, or a gnarl of sticks pointing in different directions, or images from the remnants of effigy mounds. He probably wouldn't stay in Madison long. Objects from the Driftless area kept calling him. She could see in his eyes that yearning for solitude. She tried to explain the importance of every place a person could be.

"For the longest time I thought Grandad Bluff was named for my grandfather. Sky Hi Ranch was all mine. It was only after I got older and we moved to Milwaukee that I realized the geological significance of the name. The Bluff was much bigger than my little world. That lookout post above the river held the grandfather of us all."

Mark gave her the knowing look she loved so well. They got on their bicycles to explore the relatively flat streets of Madison. Mark seemed happy to make his wheels turn. Amy didn't imagine he needed to ride his bike much at his cabin in the woods near his boyhood home. Probably once in Trempealeau, always in Trempealeau. She dreaded the next day. She had a growing sense that he would leave again for his solitary life.

Along the street next to the meadow Amy spied a single turkey, one of his tail feathers drooped at an odd angle. He was showing himself off. The turkey made bicyclists and cars swerve around him. Mark saw the turkey too and laughed: "Here is a fellow who is willing to stand his ground."

He rode ahead and found an interesting milkweed just now bursting open. He was busy catching the white fluff wishes. Amy watched many seeds floating off on their white clouds to populate the earth. Mark put some of the wishes in his bike basket, covered them with leaves for safekeeping.

"These wishes will make a border around a photograph, open up the horizon on a bluff for further exploration. I need to find a way to attach them so the wishes still fly."

Amy heard the yearn in his voice. He would need bluffs, woods, and the Mississippi to make his art open up to the world. Madison was not going to be enough. She was not going to be enough. She clutched her jacket for further closure.

The next day Mark stopped by Amy's apartment to say goodbye. Luna greeted him excitedly at the door, and he bent down to be properly introduced. Amy could see that the animal contact made him want to get back to his cats. He now kept them at his cabin.

He traveled light. The only thing he took away from his short trip to Madison was a bag of milkweed wishes. Amy knew she had gleaned something from his visit too: She saw that Mark had learned the art of how to say goodbye. The other times he had just up and gone, a bird throbbing his solitary song. That lone turkey with the askew feather came into Amy's mind. The awkward bird's effort lent a certain dignity to standing on your chosen ground.

Sure enough, the day after Mark left, Amy rode by the road where the turkey had stood against all onslaught of bikes and cars. The turkey must have found a new place to show himself off. But sitting there in the street was the one feather that wouldn't line up with the others, refusing to go on display. Amy picked up the feather and held it between her fingers as she maneuvered her bike home.

Luna had figured out that one of her main jobs was door greeter. Amy walked through the threshold of her apartment, bent down to Luna, let her sniff the turkey feather. She looked into those full moon eyes. Oh, the stories Luna's eyes began to tell. Amy would use the feather as a quill, write it all down to send to Mark and the larger universe.

Amy wondered if a photograph could ever convey sounds. She went back to focus on Mark's Grandad Bluff photograph. She saw the craggy carvings. She saw the outlines of Sky Hi Ranch. She began again to hear the thunder of hoofbeats. Then she looked deeper and distinctly heard the sounds of our elders' words echo across ancient rocks.

Coronation

After a summer and autumn of weekly trips to the Sunday farmers market Eleanor had gotten to know the local vendors by name. Louise was her favorite because she was earthy and, of all the local growers, seemed to be the proudest of her vegetables. She showed it in the tidy rows that fanned out from her canvassed stand. Sometimes a shaggy hippie helped her make change and bag the authentic bruised produce. She would throw back her brimmed hat and belly laugh, pop a sunshine cherry tomato into her upturned mouth, savor her own survival. The hippie guy often fed his gal a fistful of vegetables. Louise would crunch down on the efforts of her labors with such force that Eleanor just had to buy those green leafy lettuces, red peppers, orange carrots. At the next Sunday farmers market she noticed that the hippie helper was absent from the scene. She asked Louise where her man was.

"Gone fishin'. Rip likes the lull of a lure more than the sweat of the land. I keep him 'round because he shows me how to feel it."

Eleanor knew that a man could do that. She had allowed men into her life. One even had been good to her. She knew that rush of feeling, and was looking for a way to get back to the comfort of a good man. She grabbed her sacred sack of vegetables and made the rounds among the stalls. There was usually some kind of music at the farmer's market, men or women or both wailing away for lost love or a new tingle of desire. People in casual attire swayed to the sounds. Eleanor sat at a nearby picnic table listening, crunching down on a free ear of corn slathered in butter. The stands with cheese and honey were always popular. The squirt bears of honey called out for attention. Bee providers were busy at work in nearby fields and backyards. No product was allowed to come from far away. She learned early on that Louise's own earth source was a rented community plot near the railroad tracks just down the street. She used a large red wagon to get her produce here. No wonder everything tasted so fresh!

She circled back to Louise to say goodbye. Sometimes during the week she would see her friend working in her evolving garden down by the tracks. She counted a veritable entourage of street-wise people hovering around the rows, an ancient man carrying his albatross of grief, youths rebelling against society, the poor, the misused. She watched Louise gather them all in. She had a shoulder for anyone who needed her. By then Eleanor had learned that her gardener friend had once been a street person too. Homeless.

Eleanor started on her walk home. A sentinel of pine trees saluted hello at her back door. She leaned against one trunk and sank down to the pine needle bed of earth below. She closed her eyes and saw again Louise savor her own tomato, heard again that raucous belly laugh. She threw back her head and squirted the bear of honey into her mouth, tasted the pollination just outside her door. Life was sweet and good. She touched a fallen feather quill a bird had left for her, the communication of eons held between her weathered fingers. She took the quill inside, inspired to write a poem:

For Louise

You come back from the farmer's market
Food stamps brimming plentitude
You find yourself a heartfelt man
And rip into the entourage,

Caress the vines, embrace the vast alcove.
Your scepter hoe digs primitive refrain
Tilled garden pleasure
Burrows in your regal name.

Eleanor wondered if she should show Louise the poem. She wasn't sure how literary her friend was. Poetry made some people uncomfortable. Yet she had a strong desire to tell the queen of the vegetable plot that she was the inspiration for words growing into each other. She needed the garden poem to say that the most heartfelt written words are savory and street-wise. In her own rough raucous way Louise would understand. That next Sunday, the final farmers market of the season, Eleanor recited her poem to Louise.

"Wow. I like being called 'regal.' And I love that you got Rip into the garden!"

The days turned cold and damp. Winds blew shriveled vegetables off their stems. Then snow covered all promises of harvest. Over the winter Eleanor volunteered at the local food pantry just down the street by the railroad tracks. Sometimes she saw Louise standing in line waiting to pick up her peanut butter and canned vegetables. Food stamps spent at the grocery store went only so far in any given month. One day Eleanor saw Louise standing in line waiting and wondered out loud why Rip wasn't around to collect his own bag of food. Louise gave Eleanor her usual knowing smile.

"South for the winter. Doesn't like walls. Needs to stay warm . . . May be back for the next growing season. I listen for his knock at my door."

Eleanor kept her post in front, handing out bags for people to choose their own supplies. From way back inside the confines of canned vegetables stacked in the food pantry she heard Louise's rollicking sensual voice. Eleanor knew that bodies would be ripe all over again.

Confluence

To the States or any one of them, or any city of the States,
Resist much, obey little,
Once unquestioning obedience, once fully enslaved,
Once fully enslaved, no nation, state, city of this earth, ever
Afterward resumes its liberty.

—Walt Whitman, "To the States

Eleanor heard Louise rave about the Madison bar where people indeed explored beneath the surface of the structure, finding different ways to dive into the deep patterns in the wood. People could hide themselves away from winter blasts. Eleanor checked out the place and started spreading the word about the Union House Tavern to the people she thought might appreciate the historic establishment. She clued her friends Amy and Maddy into the bar's potential. The three friends had met Louise last summer at the local farmers market and shared an appreciation for the crispness of her vegetables.

On most days, in all seasons, primitive artist Sid Boyum, Madison's own version of Grandma Moses, sat at the bar leaning over a large drawing pad. On this winter day he was working on a caricature of a Civil War soldier. He held his art up for all to see and, in the slow-paced voice of a man who had walked the Union Corners/Atwood Avenue/Milwaukee Street corridor for years, declared his sketch to be an appropriate calling card. The soldier was marching, carrying an oversized mug of beer that was foaming into the air. His Union hat was squished on his head. Despite the soldier's seeming frivolity, Sid had sketched a look of determination on his face. Eleanor was intrigued by the reconciled disparity between frivolity and getting the job done.

She smiled at her friend Louise. Leave it to the street-smart people to know which places to go. Louise nudged her to say that the plaid shirted guy standing in front of them was the Duke of Earle, alias the owner/bartender of the drinking establishment. Louise talked about his "aliases," sat at her barstool on these cold winter days and knew he cloaked himself in many personas depending on his mood and the topic at hand.

"The Duke is an accomplished actor and can become different people: alias The Reverend, alias The Philosopher, alias The Student of History, alias The Prosecutor, alias The Masked Highwayman at Halloween."

His current ploy was lecturer in history. He proceeded to regale the ladies with the known facts of the place. Brunswick craftsmen carved the original bar and back bar, circa 1858. With reverence he explained that they made bars before they made bowling alleys. The footrail the customers used today came from the original Union House on the corner. Civil War soldiers training at Camp Randall would stop here on their way to Milwaukee or down south. They would rest their marching boots on this very rail, cash their paychecks, quaff a beer or two. The Duke confided there were rumors that in the original building the upstairs was reserved for women of the night and their gentlemen callers. In the 1950s, when the building was too decrepit to keep, the then owners moved the original wood bar, back bar, foot rail, and pictures ten feet away and built a solid brick single story structure to showcase the wealth of the past.

The Duke paused to raise a glass to those forward-looking owners. Eleanor soaked in the history. She walked over to examine the pictures on the wall. There was a detailed rendition of Camp Randall. To think that today young men played the game of football at Camp Randall Stadium! There was also an early photograph of the original two-story structure. A cow was standing casually in front. She examined the old photo, blown up and framed upon the wall: not a paved road in sight.

Eleanor sat back down on her barstool. Her hand felt the beauty of the wood. She ordered a PBR for old times' sake. The Duke smiled and nodded his approval, all the while cleaning the beer-damp wood so the ladies could lean their elbows upon the treasure. She felt an "ah" moment and knew he would be a friend. She thought of all the hands that had felt this wood.

The Duke plunked a free bowl of pretzels in front of them. He chuckled. "Salt licks." A gravel-voiced blues-man reached across Louise, seeking sustenance.

Louise let out a warning sound that got the Duke's attention. He turned to walk toward his baseball bat and the blues-man backed off. He shrugged and appeared to wait for the right time to lean in again. Louise whispered to Eleanor that the Duke had the most generous heart of anyone she knew. Then her voice expanded back out of her throat to include the people sitting on the barstools around her. The Duke had been giving away free Thanksgiving dinners for years. Street people Louise knew from a few years back arrived for the feast, then, feeling welcomed, started to hang out, anticipating the steady supply of free food the

Duke loved to cook for them. The crowd could get rowdy. The baseball bat was enough of a message.

This gregarious Duke had been interviewed on the radio about his food giveaways, his booming voice appearing on the same radio station that broadcast baseball games. The Union House had sponsored a city baseball team for years and many old teammates were loyal to the place. The players and the regulars and the street people mingled together. Sid Boyum commandeered a ringside barstool to sketch these characters for posterity. Louise let out a sigh of contentment. She seemed to be in her element. She confided to Eleanor that she had found the Union House on her own several years ago when Rip started making his winter southern migrations.

Eleanor saw this dive bar as a hidden gem. It was just the place to bring people together. The flow of the beer tap, the intermingling of the crowd, moved in the liquid of her thought. She ran her hand again over the Brunswick 1858 original surface. The past spoke to her. Women and men may have ridden to freedom here. Rumors that Union Corners was a stopping off point for the Underground Railroad persisted. They still talked about the evidence at the barber shop next door: signals of a candle in the window and the color of the clothes hung out to dry. The thought of families reuniting, riding to freedom, sent shivers through her. The hands that touched this wood had played a part in making the Underground a reality. The lucky ones who returned to Wisconsin after the Civil War would have returned to the scene of their training. Some of those same hands had been bandaged by Walt Whitman when they were out east or down south fighting for freedom. Eleanor could feel his long, flung out lines of poetry marching in the air. Her feet drum-tapped a message on the rail to conjure up the past.

Eleanor came out of her revelry in time to see Amy stride into the bar wiping the blustery cold condensation from her thick glasses. Maddy and Harry were in tow. All three had to adjust for the altered slant of light. The sun had been so bright upon the snow. The Duke of Earle greeted his new customers by passing around his business card: "proprietor, Union House, 1986-the present." His workman's hands held the history of the struggle. He saw Eleanor studying his hands. She knew they were the kind of hands Louise would appreciate too, hands that fixed what had been broken. "I was in charge of maintenance at the local steel mill. When they shut the old mill down, I bought this place." He turned his hands up and then under. Eleanor saw his calluses as a badge of honor. He gestured to surround the whole accomplishment. "Still have my tool belt hanging in the back. Comes in handy every time the dishwasher breaks."

Eleanor decided the Union House would be her winter hang out. She walked over to the jukebox, plunked some coins into the slot. She chose "Something's Got A Hold on Me." Etta James began belting it out, calling the crowd to action in the mysterious air. Eleanor then stood back to survey the scene. The song went marching, gathering the confluence of past and present. Sid Boyum was sketching rapidly. She watched Amy being her usual detective self as she examined the fossilized wood back bar with binocular vision. Eleanor too could hear the breath of life in the patterns of the wood. Maddy and Harry were riding the river between them. Eleanor dove into their undertow. She surfaced and saw Louise flirting mercilessly with that old bluesman sitting next to her. Sid Boyum held up his sketch for all to see: a picture of a drummer boy calling up the troops, elbows raised, wooden sticks tapping. Eleanor felt

Walt Whitman's "Drum-Taps" summon everyone's attention. She thought of Whitman's last words: "WARRY, SHIFT." His deathbed nurse, nicknamed Warry, had written it down. It was a request to turn him on the bed, but Eleanor always thought he also meant to shift his view from grass to the canopy sky view. She felt a shift deepen the unison of the emerging troops. The past spoke to the present. The bar had a well-worn foot rail. Take the foot off the throat. Hands could be weapons too. She thought of George Floyd murdered in Minnesota.

She remembered her husband Ray's last word when she bent over him in the ICU: "SAY." She heard the urgent surprise in his imperative. Jimi Hendrix's "Star Spangled Banner" pulsed from the jukebox. Eleanor returned to her barstool and, using the altered slant of light, continued to tell her story above the electric charged reverberation. Her hands clenched pen to paper. Her words, fists.

Playlist

Stories Inspired by Songs

1. "Say Hello": The Beatles, "Hello, Goodbye"

2. "Little Shoe Box": Louise gets her name from Bob Dylan, "Visions of Johanna "

3. "Mr. Bojangles": Jerry Jeff Walker, "Mr. Bojangles"

4. "Like a Hurricane": Neil Young, "Like a Hurricane"

5. "Respect": Aretha Franklin, "Respect"; "Think"

6. "Easy to be Hard": Three Dog Night version, "Easy to be Hard"; "Four Dead in Ohio," Crosby, Stills, Nash, and Young

7. "Magic Carpet Ride": Steppenwolf, "Magic Carpet Ride"

8. "Light After Dark": Paul and Linda McCartney, "Uncle Albert/Admiral Halsey"

9. "If Dogs Run Free": Bob Dylan, "If Dogs Run Free"

10. "The Laundry Room": The Rolling Stones thread throughout Louise's stories.

11. "Learn to Fly": The Beatles, "Blackbird"

12. "Boxcar Blues": Bob Dylan, "Absolutely Sweet Marie"

13. "Survival": Eric Burdon and The Animals, "We Gotta Get Out of This Place"

14. "Take Heed": Bob Dylan, "Boots of Spanish Leather"

15. "Start Me Up": The Rolling Stones, "Start Me Up"

16. "The Union House Tavern": John Lee Hooker, "Dimples"

17. "The Bubbler": "Strange Fruit," words and music by Abel Meeropol, as sung by Billie Holiday

18. "Troubled Eyes": Leonard Cohen, "Famous Blue Raincoat"

19. "River": Joni Mitchell, "River"

20. "Confluence": Etta James, "Something's Got a Hold on Me"; "Star Spangled Banner," Jimi Hendrix, Woodstock version

Acknowledgments

Gratefully acknowledged are the following journals, where two of the stories here previously appeared:

"Easy to be Hard" was published in *Rosebud Literary Magazine* (25th Anniversary Edition)

"Starkweather Creek" was published in *Midwest Review.*

Thank you to my editor, Christopher Chambers, who provided valuable insights on early drafts; to Dr. Ross Tangedal and the staff at Cornerstone Press, especially senior assistant editor Grace Dahl and editors Arianna Soto, Maddy Mauthe, and Brett Hill, as well as media director Zoie Dinehart, production director Carolyn Czerwinski, and sales director Nat Reiter; to Andy Millman and the writers groups at Monona Senior Center, Monona library, and Pinney library; and to Dan Eklof, "The Computer Man."

My family also deserves special mention. To my mother, Betty Skemp Curtis (1922-2023); to my sisters, Sara and Margaret, and brothers, Jim, Steve, Ken, and Ron; to my late husband, Earle Earhart (1944-2007); and to my daughter, Gwen Curtis-Earhart, and her husband, Alex Pergams. Your love and support means so much.

Jane Curtis holds a PhD from the University of Wisconsin–Madison and attended New York University on a National Endowment for the Humanities award. Her stories have been published in *Midwest Review* and the *Rosebud Literary Magazine*. She lives in southeastern Wisconsin.